U0164965

余秉楠　主编

上海三联书店

三联国际平面设计大师作品系列

[荷兰]　本·博斯

Edited by Yu Bingnan
Shanghai Joint Publishing Co.

The Selected Works of Masters of Graphic Design

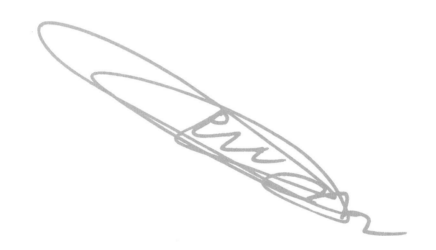

Ben Bos, edited by Yu Bingnan, translated by Gan Yilong

Copyright © 2006 by Shanghai Joint Publishing Company and Ben Bos, Amsterdam

First edition published in 2006
Shanghai Joint Publishing Company
2F, No.10, Lane 396, South Wulumuqi Road
Shanghai 200031, P.R. C.
www.sanlianc.com
ISBN 7-5426-2239-0/J·79

目　录

在法国斯特罗佩兹的大街上，1996
In the streets of St.-Tropez, France 1996

献给埃莉
For Elly

国际平面设计协会（AGI）

余秉楠

国际平面设计协会，原文为 Alliance Graphique Internationale，简称 AGI。

AGI 创建于 1951 年的法国巴黎，首任主席是法国的卡尔吕。它集中了全世界最优秀的和最有影响的著名设计师，领导着现代平面设计的潮流。

1919 年，格罗皮乌斯在德国创建了包豪斯学院。它所创造的充满生命力的现代设计风格，深刻影响着包括建筑、产品和视觉传达等诸多方面的设计。1933 年，包豪斯学院被纳粹解散，它的许多重要人物迁至英国和美国。其中巴耶尔以及在美国的其他欧洲移民莱昂尼、伯丁、宾德尔、马特、契尔尼和在英国的施勒格尔、亨利容后来成为 AGI 创建时的第一批会员。与此同时，第二次世界大战前后在平面设计领域做出杰出业绩的一个由8 位设计师组成的来自英国的天才集体被接纳为 AGI 会员。

在法国，20 世纪 30 年代最成功的海报设计师有 3 个 "C"，其中的卡尔吕和卡桑德雷，以及其后的一些优秀设计师成为会员。法国人认为文化是最优先的，设计师与画家、雕塑家一起享有声誉，得到社会的承认。因此，巴黎很自然地成为 AGI 的总部。

通常来说，当时的许多重要设计很少得到工业上的支持，人们还没有认识到设计对工业和日常生活的重要性。然而，德国的通用电器公司(AEG)和意大利的奥利维蒂打字机公司(Olivetti)显然是当时的先锋。平托利是 AGI 的第一个意大利成员，他承担了奥利维蒂的所有视觉传达设计，他的天才创意和半抽象的设计方法对于世界范围内的平面设计有着广泛的影响。

4

在瑞士，布罗克曼和霍夫曼致力于建立和发展瑞士的国际风格。由诺伊堡等人创刊的《新平面设计（*New Graphic Design*)》就是瑞士的国际风格的代表。赫德克于 1942 年创刊了《平面艺术》(*Graphic*)杂志，它在世界平面设计领域中广为流传。他们先后成为 AGI 的成员。比勒和布龙是创建 AGI 的成员，他们是杰出的海报、展示、广告的设计家，同时也是巴塞尔学校有影响的教育家。卡里吉特作为海报设计家的大师之一早已享誉远近，他在 1957 年加入 AGI。

里谢茨是 AGI 的第一个比利时成员，他为 1958 年的布鲁塞尔世界博览会所创作的海报设计使他斐声海内外。

美国的杂志设计在国际上有极高的影响力，《时代》、《生活》、《观察》等杂志建立的创意指导，在新型的传播媒体中占有重要的角色，吸引了许多一流的本地和欧洲的天才设计家，他们中的大多数人是 AGI 的成员。值得一提的还有比尔，他早在 20 世纪 30 年代就创立了典型的美国平面设计风格。

1955 年，AGI 在巴黎的卢浮宫举办首届展览，展出了来自 11 个国家的 75 位成员的作品。虽然包豪斯时期所产生的国际风格日趋明显，但由于历史的原因，展览会上各国的风格差异十分明显。仅仅在一年以后，针对 1956 年在伦敦的 AGI 展览，评论家埃尔文这样写道：" 很明显，国际风格已经统领一代潮流。"

自 1951 年 AGI 建立起，每年轮流在世界各地举行聚会（1973 年由于中东战争取消了在耶路撒冷的会议），会员们在友好和相互尊重的气氛中，进行认真和富有成果的学术探讨，举办会员作品展览，培训有才干的平面设计大学生和青年设计师，并用平面设计的方法帮助世界各国的企业、公司和它们的跨国组织的发展。

1969 年，AGI 将总部从巴黎迁至瑞士的苏黎世。目前，AGI 除了上述国家的会员外，还有德国、澳大利亚、加拿大、捷克、丹麦、芬兰、伊朗、以色列、日本、墨西哥、荷兰、挪威、波兰、西班牙、瑞典、韩国和中国的约 300 名会员，清华大学美术学院（原中央工艺美术学院）的余秉楠于 1992 年被接纳为 AGI 的第一个华人会员。2004 年 AGI 年会在北京举办，这是该组织首次在中国举办年会。

AGI 作为各国著名设计师的联合组织，是国际平面设计界的权威组织，在国际上享有崇高的声誉。

Alliance Graphique Internationale (AGI)
Yu Bingnan

Alliance Graphique Internationale, abbreviated as AGI, was founded in 1951 in Paris, France. Its first president was Carlu from France. Among its ranks are the most outstanding and influential famous designers worldwide. It leads since then the trends of the modern graphic design.

In 1919, Gropius founded Bauhaus in Germany. The modern design style developed by Bauhaus deeply influenced many creations in the fields of architecture, industrial products and visual communication. After Bauhaus was closed by the Nazis in 1933, many of its teachers fled Germany and worked in Britain or the United States. Some of them, e.g. Bayer, along with other emigrates such as Lionni, Burtin, Binder, Matter, Tscherny in the United States and Schleger, Henrion in Britain became the first members of AGI. At the same time, a talented body of eight British designers, who had proved their worth before and during the war, became eligible members.

In France, the most successful poster designers in the Thirties of the last century were the three Cs. Two of them, Carlu and Cassandre, together with other excellent designers afterwards, were members of AGI. Art and artists have been always much respected by the French people. Like painters and sculptors, designers in France enjoy a reputation and an acknowledged place in society. It was, therefore, natural that Paris became the new AGI headquarters.

Generally speaking, around that time many important designs are not supported by the industry, which means the important effect of design on industrial and daily life had not been realized. AEG in Germany and Olivetti Typewriter in Italy, however, played a pioneer role in this aspect. Pintori, the first Italian AGI member, was responsible for all the visual communication of Olivetti. His imaginative and semi-abstract approach became a worldwide influence on graphic design.

In Switzerland M ü ller-Brockmann and Hofmann were instrumental in evolving and establishing the Swiss approach internationally. "New Graphic Design", of which Neuburg was a founder member, became the mouthpiece of the new Swiss International Style. Herdeg started "Graphis" magazine in 1942. This covered graphic design worldwide, with a much more general approach. Both of them were received as members of AGI. BüHer and Brun, the two founder members of AGI, had been well-established designers of posters, exhibitions and advertising and both were influential teachers at the Basel School. Carigiet was already well known as one of the masters of posters. He was made an honorary member in 1957.

Richez is the first Belgic member of AGI. His poster for the Brussels

World Exhibition has brought him international reputation.

American magazine design became highly influential on an international scale. "*Time*", "*Life*", "*Look*" established the creative art director of a magazine as the most important figure in this new communication medium. Magazine design in the United States attracted the best native and European talent. The majority of these art directors were AGI members. Special mention here must be made of Beall who had created a typical USA graphic style as early as the Thirties of the last century.

At the first AGI exhibition at the Louvre in Paris in 1955, at which the work of seventy-five designers from eleven countries was shown, although the International Style, existent since the Bauhaus, had become more important, but the national characteristics of most were evident in the exhibits, for the historic reasons given. Only one year later, however, when referring to the 1956 London exhibition, the critic Elvin stated: "Clearly the International Style had begun to dominate the scene."

Since the foundation in 1951 AGI holds assembly meeting every year in different places all over the world (except the meeting 1973 in Jerusalem due to the Middle East crises). In a friendly atmosphere members discussed seriously but fruitfully issues of graphic design, held exhibitions of their works, trained talented students and young designers in this field, and helped with their experiences enterprises, companies and their joint ventures all over the world.

In 1969 AGI has moved headquarter from Paris to Zurich in Switzerland. Along with the members from the countries mentioned above, AGI has at present around 300 members from Germany, Australia, Canada, Czech, Denmark, Finland, Iran, Israel, Japan, Mexico, Netherlands, Norway, Poland, Spain, Sweden, Korea and China. Yu Bingnan of the Academy of Arts & Design, Tsinghua University, has become the first Chinese AGI member in 1992. The 2004 AGI Congress was held in Beijing and it is also the first time the AGI Congress was held in China.

As a Network of famous designers from all over the world, AGI is an authoritative association worldwide in graphic design, which enjoys high reputation internationally.

双重天赋

我的一部分童年在第二次世界大战中希特勒占领下的阿姆斯特丹度过。中学和父母健在的家是两个仅存的安全的地方 —— 在如此阴森的环境下没有比这更安全的了。我的父亲是第二代装订工。在我家里，尊重纸张是神圣的规矩。家里有足够的纸张激起了我强烈的绘画的愿望。中学艺术教师注意到我的天赋，给我在教室里充分的自由。一台打字机，一只奢侈的35毫米柯达照相机（荷兰解放后不久一个海员外甥送给我的礼物）是基本的工具，以使我能开始一个写作、插图说明、"设计"和编辑各种各样的书面纸张的"生涯"。我的"生涯"是为同学、我的运动俱乐部、本国军人和阿尔卑斯俱乐部而服务的。他们后来称我是双重天赋的报纸从业人员。杂志和报纸使我能回想起我生命中的爱。我在荷兰空军服役当军官时参加了记者教程。

受雇于阿赫恩德贸易公司时，我当了他们个人杂志的记者兼设计。后来我花了十五年的时间训练了整整一代荷兰同事，教他们记者专业课程：形式与内容。阿赫恩德是我交流思想方面第一个重要的雇主（1954–1963）。我先是做他们的广告文字撰写人，同时发展了作为概念制作者、设计者和艺术指导方面的技巧。在阿姆斯特丹平面造型高中和里埃特维德学院的六年晚班为我打下了基础，使我能进入那时还年轻的平面造型设计的职业生涯。学院里我的主要的老师、设计师

威姆·克鲁威尔，以及他在阿赫恩德团体的同事，工业产品设计师弗里索·克拉默，参与建立了荷兰第一个多学科设计团体 —— "全体设计"，该团体建立于1963年。他们选我领导他们的画室雇员，但不久我有机会建立我自己的设计团队。我的教育背景（带有文学和经济学课程的中学教育）加上在阿赫恩德的实践经历，使许多商业倾向的客户把他们的方案交给我和我的设计团队来制作。三年以后，他们任命我为全体设计的创意指导。我在这个团体中呆了二十八年。

六十年代中期，公司特征的专业化很快发展为一个主要是设计的问题。我在这些活动中是专家，做过很多这些规划。这些规划构成了全体设计持续运作的强劲的经济支柱。由于这是一个新的领域，特征方案的规则和"基础"只能由先驱设计者创造。作为公司特征的设计者和"报纸从业人员"，这个经历使我赢得了国际声誉。我在设计出版社出版了几本有关这些主题的书籍和许多文章。我经常在全世界很多研讨会、艺术学校和大学作讲演。1978年，我经挑选受邀成为国际平面设计协会（AGI）的成员。1996年，布尔诺两年一届会议接纳我为荣誉会员。1998年，我又成为荷兰设计者协会（BNO）的荣誉成员。在多次设计竞赛和考试中我都担任裁判，在荷兰是如此，在国外也是如此。我的作品在个人展和团体活动中都有展出。在国内外，我频频得奖。在同行里，我

常常被称作"公司特征设计的权威"。

这些规划使我有机会设计了大约120个商标，其中很多存在了几十年。1998年，我获得了一个世界商标设计奖，同时获奖的还有设计者米尔顿·格拉色、罗尔夫·哈德、尤金·格罗斯曼、恩斯特·罗克、所尔·巴斯、约瑟夫·牡勒－布罗克曼和依科·田中。

我重新设计了两份荷兰国家报纸："阿尔机敏·汉德斯布拉德"和"亥特·巴罗尔"。为第一份，我也开发了一种创新的方法把新闻传送到原始的宽版面，但为了所有读者的方便也可用小版面。不幸的是，这个"汉德斯布拉德"不久后和另一份有质量的报纸"NRC"在我的方法实施之前合并了。我为这份新的报纸设计了报头。

在我的代表作选集里有两个客户占首要地位。兰德斯塔德雇佣服务集团在它早年时（1967年）就找我了，那时还只是一个小规划。这个集团飞速增长，成了世界同行中的领导者。三十多年里，我为他们在很多国家设计并监督他们的视觉标志。

在交流领域中阿赫恩德是我的第一个雇佣者，他成了"全体设计"和"设计 II"（我自己的设计团队，成立于1991年）的客户。我和阿赫恩德的

关系持续了五十年，当中有过间断。最近的规划中有他们的一个"模比里厄姆"，即他们的办公室用具的室内博物馆样式的设计。

1993年，我建立了 NAGO，荷兰平面造型设计档案馆，收集了自第二次世界大战到目前为止许多荷兰杰出的平面造型设计者的有创造力的作品。2000年，我的专著《本·博斯一生的设计》由阿姆斯特丹 BIS 出版，有荷兰语和英语两种版本。它与布雷达的一个叫"德·比亚德"的博物馆回顾展协同出版。

2002年，我为荷兰平面造型设计文化基金会写了他们的年度书，题目是《你认为我是谁》。其主题是"特征"。我的妻子埃莉作了图片研究，同时在因特网上收集了许多特别的信息。这本书被选进了"年度最佳50榜"。

很多年以来我一直就公司特征为不同的专业课程作讲演。在九十年代后期，我一直在鹿特丹伊茨塞斯学院教平面设计的历史，并帮助这个学院设计管理新研究领域规划。

本·博斯
国际平面设计协会

9

Doubly gifted, they say

Part of my boyhood took place during the second world war, in Amsterdam, occupied by Hitler's army. The secondary school and the parental home were the only 'safe' places - as safe as those can be under such grim circumstances. My father was a second generation bookbinder by trade. Respect for paper was a 'holy' house rule. Enough paper at the family home to stimulate my strong urge to draw. The art-master at the secondary school recognized the talent and gave me total freedom in the classroom. A typewriter and the luxury of a Kodak 35mm camera (a gift from a seafaring nephew, just after the liberation of Holland) were the essential tools to start a 'carreer' of writing, illustrating, 'designing' and editing all kinds of papers. F or the schoolmates, for my athletics club, for the national servicemen as well as for the Alpine Club. They would later call me a doubly gifted newspaper man. Magazines and papers would remain the love of my lifetime. I took a course in jounalism during my compulsory service as an officer in the Dutch Airforce.

When employed with the trading-firm Ahrend, I became the journalist/designer of their personnel magazine. Later I trained over a period of 15 years a whole generation of Dutch colleagues in this journalistic specialism: form and content. Ahrend was my first important employer in communications (1954-1963). I started with them as their copywriter, but developed my skills as a concept maker, designer and art director. Six years of evening classes at the Amsterdam Graphic high school and the Rietveld Academy prepared me for the next step

into the then still young profession of graphic design. My most dominating academy teacher, the designer Wim Crouwel, and his colleague at the Ahrend Group, industrial designer Friso Kramer, were among the founding partners of the first Dutch multi-discipline design group 'Total Design', thatstar ted off in 1963. They chose me to lead their studio employees, but very soon I got the chance to start my own design team. The combination of my educational background (a secondary school with a literary/economic program) and my practical experience with Ahrend meant that many projects from business-oriented clients found their way to my drawing table and design team. After three years they appointed me as a creative director of Total Design. I would eventually stay with this design group for 28 years.

The mid-sixties were the years in which the specialism of Corporate Identity rapidly developed into a major design issue. I specialized in this field of activitiy and was in charge of numerous of these projects.They constituted a strong financial backbone for the continuity of Total Design's operations. Because it was such a new sphere of work, the rules and the 'grammer' of identity programs had to be invented by the pioneering designers. My work as a corporate identity designer and a 'newspaper man' established my international repuation. I published several books on these subjects and numerous articles in the design press. I was also a regular lecturer at seminars, art schools and universities all over the world.
In 1978 I was invited to be a member of the select Alliance Graphique Internationale (AGI). In 1996 the

Brno Biennale made me an honorary member. The same happened in 1998 when I became an honorary member of the Dutch Designers' Association BNO. I was a judge at many design competitions and examinations,in the Netherlands and abroad. My work has been exhibited in one-man-shows as well as during group events. I was awarded frequently at home or abroad. Within the profession I am often called 'a guru of corporate identity design'.

The projects gave me the opportunity to design some 120 logotypes, many of which survived for decades. I was given a World Logotype Design Award 1998, in the good company of designers like Milton Glaser, Rolf Harder, Eugene Grossman, Ernst R och, Saul Bass, Josef Müller-Brockmann and Ikko Tanaka.

I redesigned two Dutch national newspapers, the 'Algemeen Handelsblad' and 'Het Parool'. For the first one I also developed an innovative plan to present the news on the original broad sheet forat, but with all the readers' comfort of a tabloid paper. Unfortunately this Handelsblad merged soon after that with another quality paper, 'NRC', even before my plan was implemented. For this new national newspaper I designed the masthead.

Two clients took a dominating role in my portfolio. The Randstad employment service group came to me in it's early years (1967), as a small project. The group underwent an enormous growth, to become one of the world leaders in it's trade. I designed and super vised their visual identity for more than 30 years and in many countries.

Ahrend, my first employer in the field of communications, came back as a client of Total Design and of FORMatie2 (my own design team, founded after I had left Total Design in 1991).The relationship with Ahrend covered - be it with some interruptions - a period of 50 years. One of the final projects was the making of their 'Mobilium', a in-house museum of their office furniture design.

In 1993 I founded NAGO, the Netherlands Graphic Designers' Archive, which by now took care of the creative heritage of many outstanding Dutch graphic designers since the second world war. In 2000 my monography 'Ben Bos Design of a Liftetime' was published by BIS Amsterdam, in a Dutch and an English version. It was published in conjuction with a retrospective exhibition in Museum 'de Beyerd', Breda.

In 2002 I wrote for the Dutch Foundation for Graphic Culture their annual book, entitled 'Who do you think I am?' The subject was 'Identities'. My wife Elly did the picture research and collected also a lot of special information from the internet. The book was elected among the '50 Best of the Year'.

For many years I have been lecturing about Corporate Identity for various professional courses. During the late nineties I was teaching the history of graphic design at the Ichthus College Rotterdam, where I also assisted in planning its new field of study for design managers.

Ben Bos AGI BNO

11

Twenty first century

XXI

二十一世纪

14

you

europe
2020
yourope

you eu

15

20
20

16

Ahrend Mobilium

ahrend

De firma Weduwe J.Ahrend & Zoon
werd in 1896 opgericht.
Ahrend ontwikkelde zich zeer snel tot
een succesvol handels- en reproductiebedrijf.
Oprichter Jacobus Ahrend (1875-1956)
was in 1896 vanwege zijn leeftijd
nog niet 'teken- en handelingsbevoegd'.
Dus 'leende' hij de naam van zijn moeder,
de Weduwe.
Dat deed de zaken geen kwaad.

Het stalen meubel maakte zijn intrede
aan het einde van de jaren '20.
'Doe Meer' stoelen voor kantoorarbeid
werden eerst uit Engeland geïmporteerd.
Met de meubelfabriek Oda in St.-Oedenrode,
eigendom van de familie Van de Kamp,
ontstond een vaste samenwerking in 1932.
De stalen kasten en bureaus kwamen
voornamelijk daar vandaan.
Twee jaar later werd ook de band met
Jan Schröfer, oprichter van meubelfabriek
'de Cirkel' (Amsterdam, later Zwanenburg)
gesmeed.
'de Cirkel' produceerde lange tijd vooral
stoelen en andere meubels op basis van
gebogen stalen buis.

艺术家玛里基克·德·科伊的商标，2000
Logotype for artist Marijke de Goey, 2000

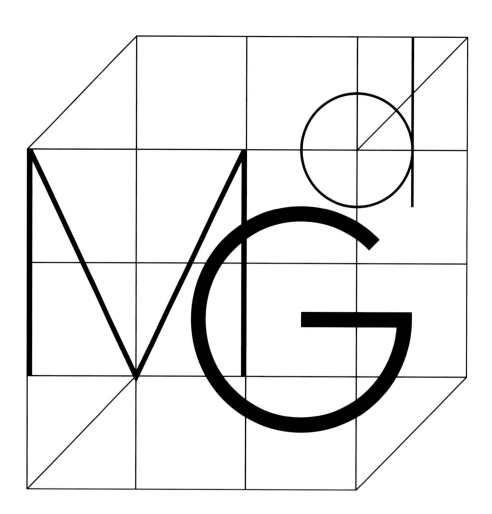

18

19

Paris, un amour éternel

Ben Bos, Pays-Bas

国际平面设计协会 AGI，巴黎大庆会议海报，2001
Alliance Graphique Internationale AGI, poster for Paris jubilee congress, 2001

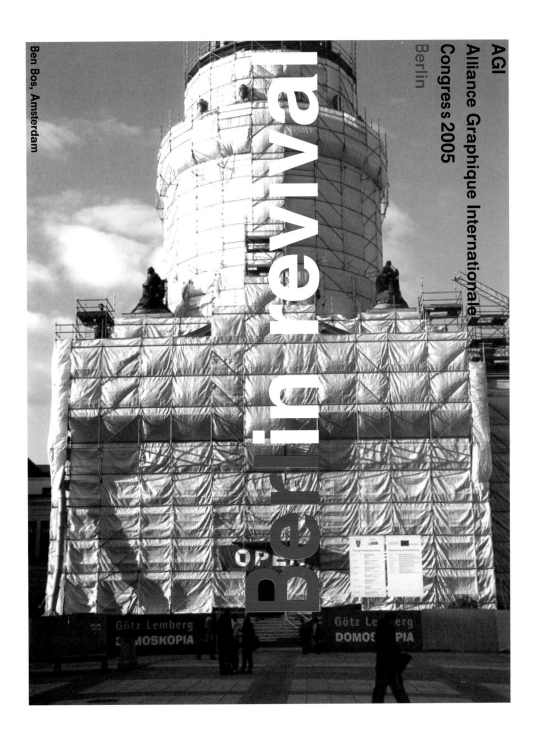

柏林 AGI 大会 2005 海报 (独创——黑色)
Poster for Berlin, AGI congress 2005 (original in black only)

22

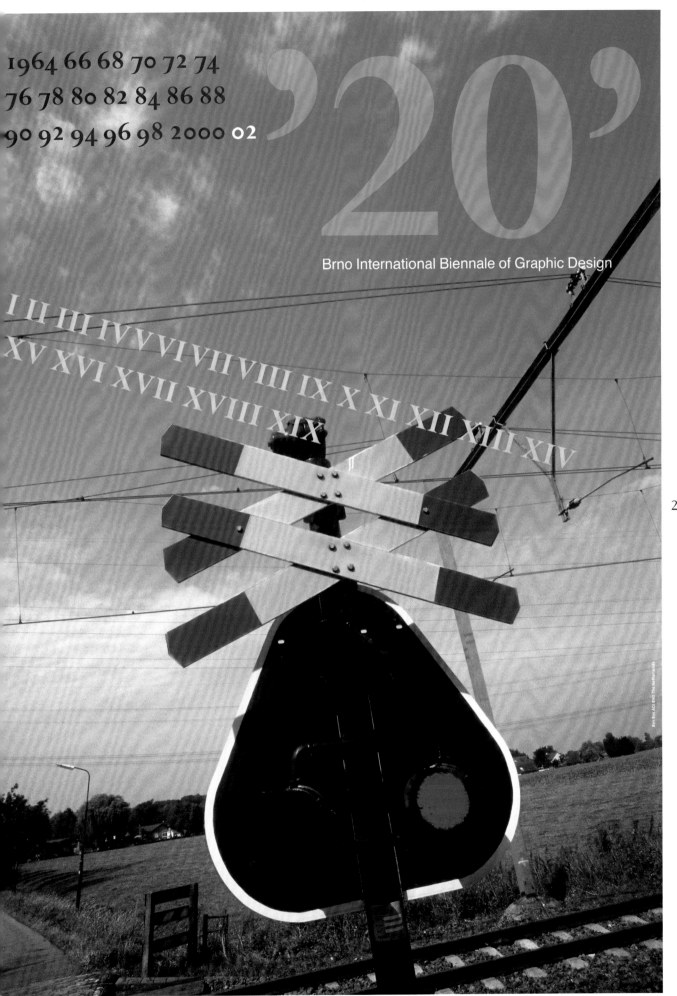

1964 66 68 70 72 74 76 78 80 82 84 86 88 90 92 94 96 98 2000 02

'20'

Brno International Biennale of Graphic Design

I II III IV V VI VII VIII IX X XI XII XIII XIV XV XVI XVII XVIII XIX

23

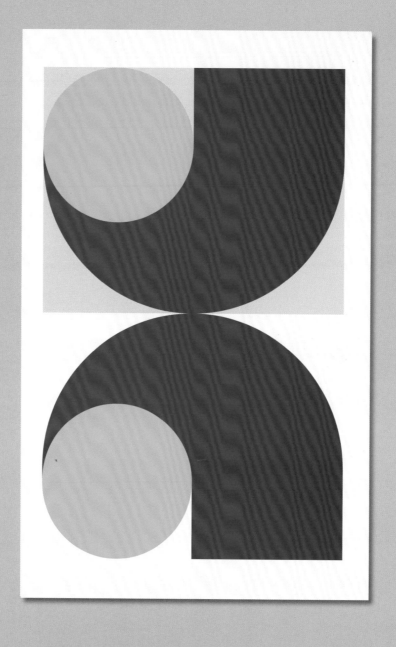

humanity
philanthropy
fairness
dedication

ASIA
DELHI
CALCUTTA
RANGOON
MADRAS

25

It's a weird world.   We leven in een dwaze wereld.
So watch your steps in   Pas goed op jezelf in

2004

EllyBonsenBenBos

贺卡，2004
Greeting card 2004

"全体设计"东京展览海报，2004
Poster for Tokyo exhibition Total Design, 2004

HUIS

Huisstijl is een Noodzakelijk Goed.
Het kost geld, maar de duurste huisstijl is géén huisstijl.

STIJL

ISBN 90-6369-033-9

9 789063 690335 >

Ben Bos

HUIS

de kern van de zaak

STIJL

B*I*S

关于印刷风格和公司特征的书，包括文章和设计，200

Book about housestyle / corporate identity. Text and design, 200

Persoonlijk logo uit de jaren '30
van Piet Zwart, Nederlands ontwerppionier
met wereldreputatie.

关于印刷风格和公司特征的书，包括文章和设计，200

Book about housestyle / corporate identity. Text and design, 200

isstijl is in wezen soms zoiets als *His Masters' Voice*

32

Twentieth century

XX

二十世纪

Back to the

50's

回到五十年代

阿赫恩德个人杂志封面，1959
Covers for Ahrend personnel magazine, 1959

在里埃特维德学院学习，1956–1961
Studying at the Rietveld Academy, 1956-1961

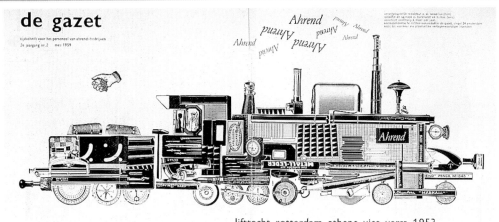

为阿赫恩德做照片模特的本·博斯（由简·福厄斯内尔拍摄）1959
Ben Bos as a photomodel for Ahrend (photography Jan Versnel) 1959

38

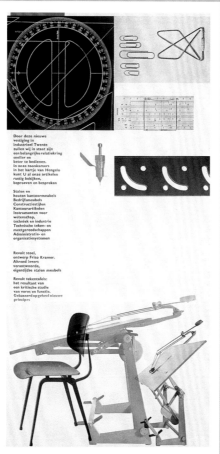

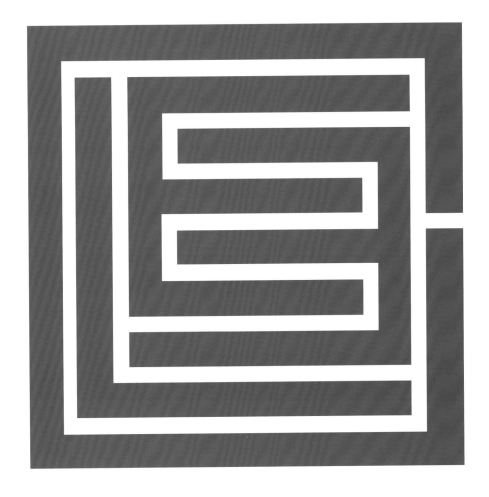

39

范・李，保险顾问，商标，1960
Van Lee, insurance consultants, logotype, 1960

40

"尽管博斯自称是一个功能主义者，他相信他比他的老师(威姆·克罗威尔)使用功能主义更宽广的定义。这由他接受的几个任务而产生。从1957年到1991年，他为Hulp voor Onbehuisden[帮助无家可归者]工作。博斯写作和设计了宣传小册子，编辑了几个机构的杂志。在一个工程队里，他工作了两年，其目的是为老年人之家Nieuw Vredenburgh (一个任务，开始于路线系统，其后广泛地牵涉到建筑师范·坚特和穆赫斯塔夫的内部绘画)。其目的是再次加入热情、适居性和由此而产生的人性化。"

——德克·范·金克尔，记者兼作者

"当他还是学生时，本通过他的奉献成名。他的获得多种技能的决心深深打动了我。我欣赏他的多才多艺：他能像专家一样画画、拍照，更不用说他的设计的感觉。他使我感到我已经没有什么可以教他的了。"

"……和我一样，本欣赏瑞士印刷家。他们真正知道少就是多。本是这种态度的持有者，我也常想持有它。然而，如果把我的作品同他的相比，我的更枯涩更简单。本的全部作品想象丰富，色彩绚丽，热情奔放。他有一种美化事物并布置它们的爱好。"

"……我认为，在《Mode en module》(关于我的一本书)描述中，把本说成是追随者——永远的追随者，这是错误的。他是一个了不起的设计者，他有他自己的特征。他为"全体设计"的工作是无价的，他保证了它的持续性和经济上的安全性。然而，他的重要性远不只这些……"

——威姆·克罗威尔，本在学院时的老师，后来在"全体设计"时的搭档

"本·博斯的作品清澈明晰，反映了全体设计的理想，实践了画室所鼓吹的信条。那就是说，他不是一个艺术家，而是一个真正的工具设计者。对于全体设计来说，本等价于为他所塑的金身。"

——安松·比克，设计者，全体设计的前搭档

"我把本看作是一个大师。我从他那里学到了很多，尽管他没有教我怎样。然而，我在我的位置上看到他许多，他的设计的方式、他的工作的方法、做事的的方法。这是一种非常专业的方法，我很欣赏。他能写、能照相、能专业的设计和说明。他做事有很多概念，并能体现在具体细节上。他又做了占篇幅的设计，有大有小，在这个意义上，我把他看作一个全能的设计者，与皮耶特·茨瓦特是一个层次：一个有紧迫感、有感情的复兴派，能做任何事。"

——约斯特·克林肯伯格，本的设计队伍的一员，1980–1987

"公司渴望以程式化的面目和相应的商标出现在世人面前，这导致了无尽的商标的潮流。这一发展开始于1970年左右，相当抽象的标记，终极简单化的信息，多少占主导地位。设计职业有一种新的象征的语言。不久，人们看到，在工业化世界里，人们用几乎相同的口径说话：同样的几何图形在另外的地方由意趣相同的人同时制造出来。但事实还不止如此。这个发展最终导致了后来商标地位的提升，这使得独创性和分化性很容易达到。在这空前动态的年代里，各种机构面临着不确定的未来，商标名不能维持长久。战略联盟、合并、接管或者破产缩短了许多公司特征的预期寿命。我们为客户建议的设计曾经打算维持十到二十年；但现在事实上不可能找到敢看到那么远的企业家。商标保持了我们的图象文化中的独特的一面，而且存在得很好。"

——本·博斯

(本文是萨门威肯德·温特威帕斯的《特征的进化》一书中本·博斯所写介绍的一部分，出版于阿姆斯特丹，2000)

……"本·博斯为'德·比简科夫'百货商店制作的设计是他的设计方法的典型的一例。个人杂志、包装、标识、酒类纸夹和购物袋经常有一种顽皮的或说明性的作用使印刷品更为吸引人。博斯发现了这一点，并实际应用于爱因德侯文百货商店导购图上的自动扶梯直观画中颜色和图画方式。"

——赫布·赫本，de Volkskrant (国家早报)

41

Quotes

'Although Bos calls himself a functionalist, he believes he uses a broader definition of Functionalism than his teacher (Wim Crouwel). That was also borne out by several commissions that he accepted. From 1957 to 1991 he worked for Hulp voor Onbehuisden [Aid for the Homeless]. Bos wrote and designed begging folders and edited the organizations' magazine. He also worked for two years in the construction team for the old people's home Nieuw Vredenburgh, a commission that started with a routingsystem and led to a far-reaching involvement with the interior drawings by the architects Van Gendt & Mühlstaf. Once again the objective was to add warmth, livability and thereby humanity.'

Dirk van Ginkel, journalist/writer

'Even when he was still a student, Ben distinguished himself through his great dedication. I was quite impressed by his determination to acquire various skills. I also admired him for his versatility: he could draw, photograph and write like the best, not to speak of his feeling for design. He was someone who gave me the feeling that there was nothing left for me to teach him'.

'...Like myself, Ben admired the Swiss typographers. They really understood that Less is More. Ben was a great adherent of that approach and I too have always aimed to achieve that. However, if I compare my work to his, mine is much drier and more straightforward. Ben's oeuvre is imaginative, colourful and lyrical. He has a penchant of making things beautiful and arranging them.'

'...I believe that the description in Mode en module, the book that was written about me, of Ben as a follower, the eternal follower-up, is mistaken. He is a marvellous designer who has his own identity. His work for Total Design was invaluable, even if only because he guaranteed its continuity and financial security. But his importance is much greater than that...'

Wim Crouwel, Ben's teacher at the academy and later his partner in Total Design

'With the clarity of his designs Ben Bos carried the ideal of Total Design and really put into practice the gospel that the studio preached. That is to say, he did not work as an artist, but as a genuinely instrumental designer. Ben was worth his weight in gold to Total Design'.

Anthon Beeke, designer, formerly a partner in Total Design

'I view Ben as a master. I have learnt a lot from him, although he hasn't taught me much. However I was in a position to see a lot of him, his approach of design, his working methods, the way he did things. It was a professional approach that I admired. He could write, was a good photographer, an expert designer and illustrator. He had a way with concepts and was clearly present in the details. He also made good spatial designs, both on the large and small scale, and in that sense I consider him an all-round designer, on a level with Piet Zwart: a driven and emotional Renaissance man who can turn his hand on anything.'

Joost Klinkenberg, a member of Ben's design team, 1980-'87

'The corporate desire to present a stylised front with matching logos has led to a virtually endless flow of logos and trademarks. When the development really took off around 1970, the fairly abstract sign, the ultimate simplification of the message, more or less predominated. The design profession had a new figurative language. And it soon became apparent that many others throughout the industrialized world spoke in roughly the same tongue: the same often rather geometric shapes were produced simultaneously by the like-minded elsewhere. And that was not the idea. This eventually led to the subsequent upgrading of the trademark, making originality and differentiation easier to achieve.
In this age of unprecedented dynamism organizations face uncertain futures and brand names are less durable. Strategic alliances, mergers, take-overs or bankruptcy cut short the life expectations of many corporate identities. The designs we once proposed to our clients were intended to last for 10 or 20 years; now it is virtually impossible to find entrepreneurs who dare look that far ahead. The trademark or logo however remains a characteristic aspect of our 'image culture' and as such is definitely here to stay.'

Ben Bos (part of his introduction to a book on 'Identity in progress' by Samenwerkende Ontwerpers, Amsterdam, 2000)

....' The work Ben Bos made for the department store 'de Bijenkorf' is a typical example of his design approach. The personnel magazine, packaging, labels, wine folders and shoppingbags often have a playful and/or illustrative touch that heightens the attractiveness of the printed matter. Bos finds that in the use of colour, in a drawing or the way he visualizes the escalator on the routingmap of the store at Eindhoven'.

Hub. Hubben, de Volkskrant (national morning paper)

42

Further in the

60's

六十年代更进一步

全体设计管理会议，1963：迪克.施瓦兹，弗列索.克雷默，贝诺.威辛，保罗.施瓦兹，本.博斯，威姆.克罗威尔
Management meeting Total Design, 1963: Dick Schwarz, Friso Kramer, Benno Wissing, Paul Schwarz, Ben Bos, Wim Crouwel

在工作，1969
At work, 1969

摄影 简.厄斯内尔
Photography JanVersnel

44

HVO（帮助无家可归者），商标，1969
HVO(Aid for the Homeless)，logotype 1969

46

rembrandtpfann 47

48

阿尔格拉斯，建筑用玻璃，商标，1964
Alglas, glass building-materials, logotype, 1964

德·比简科夫，商标礼物服务，1967
de Bijenkorf, logo Gift Services, 1967

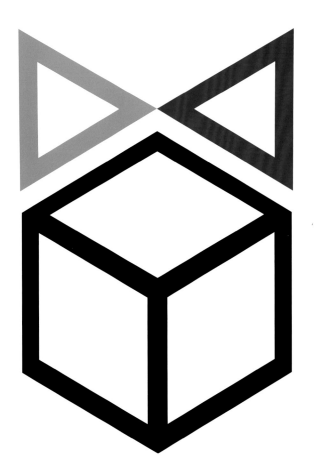

49

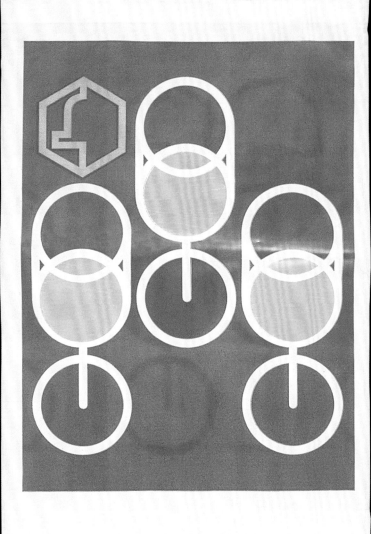

de Bijenkorf

· 比简科夫，酒类购物袋，1967
Bijenkorf, carrier bag for wines, 1967

德 · 比简科夫，唱片购物袋，1969
de Bijenkorf, carrier bag for records, 1969

德·比简科夫，母亲节海报 1965
de Bijenkorf, Mother's Day poster 1965

德·比简科夫，"萨默科夫"购物袋，1966
de Bijenkorf, shopping bag 'Summerkorf', 1966

52

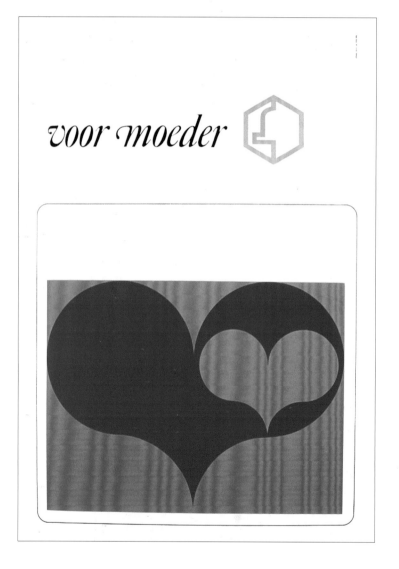

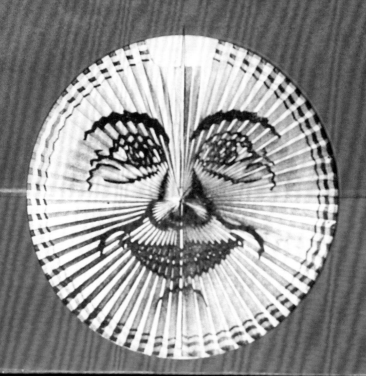

De grootste revolutie van alle campings is er in buiten Europa. Toverhuislaan met nog een extra gevel die bestaat. Niet zo vertrouwd eigenlijk, dat de ANWB in de Kampeerkampioen veel aandacht besteedde aan deze combi... Twee losse tenten worden samen zeereen dubbel waardevol! Wat is de Toverhuislaar?

toverhuislaar

1

bodem

+ 1 = 3

Wilde Kameraija

Wilde Wingard

Een deel de Bijenkorf exclusief ontwikkelde kampeertent, die samen met de bubbeltjes halfzeten Bodem, de (dingenoomig) Wilde Kameraija of de (voorpertuning) Wilde Wingard ene nieuwe vormt. In de achterwand van de Toverhuislaar is nl. een uitsparing aangebracht, die daarin aandlichit aansluit aan de voorhuif van de Bodem, de Kameraija en de Wingard. Hierdoor ontstaat een 'indurmid' huisg, de disappleateen zijn omresso in de huidoom. Daar liggig een dendin tent te neenen- is bepaald mal overdeuven, de huing meist naar refet 360 x 320 cm.

ontwerd volgens het bekende de Bijenkorf principe en uit de al in onse tentkkotlectie dinter kunst van Calla... vool speldeden. toderueen, lengende van de... len reten rteen van de vorkkuijle Zefs de prijs van de Toverhuislaar is sensa... ..eel, sompelsel. 198.—
En ze en ook nopipjaabegiifjen de Toverhuislaar... Toverhuislaar + bessenaoon croons Boldenk 198.— + 149.— 347.—
Toverhuislaar + droppnops croons Wilde Kameraaja... 198.— + 199.— 353.—

Wie zo gelukkig is, zi' een Boldenk of Wilde Kampel je te beullen, kan dus voor ze nog geen 350.— deze hui tent verheer tot een dri- tent!

Vlieg met adv-roende de Bijenkorf zl, sioest voer le beselten. De pris niu de advies eigenlijk nog den- geester meet een in-ze naj de belangstelling- ele prins en de enthousiastc verbalen van de Toverhu- anlaar oochters 1968, moet op een keer den overstel- pande belangstelling wor- den-gerekend!

347.—

377.—

285.—

BOTEN

Sportyak

Sportyak vaaanboot. Robotboot of zeilboot aannekka je op de wagen wat je neemn en het luht, onet 317 kg- Drag- mohat 317 kg- lung 212 cm, breed 108 cm- uitligeuule bodem en onder- das onarkkoot special bodemprofiel zorgt dat materiale stabilitiet silvethyten dus voor veel plaunzar besimkerd. 036.—

Midenroan	19.50
Gaffeleun	9.50
Bankje	9.50
Noalsen roeinienen	16.50

Zeilsens. Stoil te demoteren, kien- op te leggen- Met prosibel fuk en rozaardon plus alumnuge ram met sl- standbediening. 458.—

Speciaal ontwerpen voor de Bijenkorf en gebouwd door Fransku gnootsde satern- bouwer. Vastvulding getest. dilentig trefuheu wage nylon zijwanden en opvaudwve houten vloer en schokbed te- veitoen. Complet met bui- tenboordmotuu. De pris ene zlemene verdrading 288.— Loase hussertt 58.50 roeitamen 37.50
Snelle 1-persoonskano met flinke zitvuimte. Heel stabiel 78.50

Snelle 2-persoonskano met flinke zitruimte Heel stabiel 185.—

Eurovinylboten van PVC- met nigelbouwde pomp, op- blaasbare bodem, reddings- lijn random, zekering en nalrdubbeveiliging- inclupf opblogbass Halon- 4-persuns serne ene Mary 115.— 75.—

Oplblaasbore eonpersoons- boot. Vliet berefft voorzog- ving en stabiliet bennkend op flinke snelheid 19.50

56

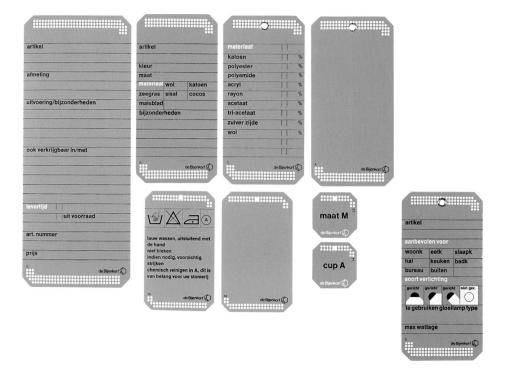

57

58

a sketch or two, which I then blow up to the required size. In the computerized age I did not decide to do the keyboard job myself: I work with an expert operator (use his knowlegde, his equipment, his state-of-the-art hardware and always up-dated software) and I just sit with him and dictate my ideas. In most cases I even don't confront the operator with a real sketch on paper. It's all in my head, when we start the dictation. The great advantage of the computer is however that nowadays I will change my mind more easily about details. The client does not get my first version -like in the old days- but one that has been reconsidered in various aspects.

Being a keen photographer myself, often taking myself the pictures I needed for my commissions - I strongly believe in the communicative power of black & white photography. Since colour pictures are nowadays used for advertising even the cheapest products, black & white can represent a special 'elite' quality, where the accent lies entirely on shapes and the essence of the subject itself, without a distraction by often overwhelming colours. This does not mean a complete denial of good, high quality colour photography; but as colours are now 'mainstream', contrastful black & white has for me a kind of noblesse and special attractiveness.

The grid has been a dominating tool in my work as well. Although that meant that my works have a distinct form of organisation, I do not exclude the use of attractive 'ornaments'; my works are not cold or severe. Nor do I see the grid as an absolute straightjacket; if necessary I liberate myself from its pattern. In the early years of my work at Total Design grids were still a novelty and had to be explained to

would lead to dull, too obvious design solutions. I then made a 16mm movie that showed them the really infinite possibilities of a rather simple grid, which I used for the small-sized employee's monthly for my client De Bijenkorf, the leading Dutch department stores. It showed that I could make so many page variations that they would, being laid side by side, easily surround the whole length of the Equa

The values of my designs depend on a perfect balanc between all components of the designed product. Thi means that content of the text is as important as the typography or the use of colours and paper, as well as the quality of printing and binding. I was never a designer who chose for expensive solutions. My work were never meant to become a kind of statues for my own fame. I prefer to address the final user in an hon easily understandable way. I am always aware of the fact that any piece of communication is constantly in competition with many other pieces. I never denied m own political or ethical convictions. I would not work 'the enemy', not for the kind of people I couldn't trust respect. Choosing for such an approach of my professional responsibilty resulted quite often in longlasting friendly relationships with my clients.

Many good colleagues and assistants with whom I worked in my team at Total Design stayed with me fo a long period; I owe them a lot of respect. I remained often involved in their later careers and plans. Having been a member of the Alliance Graphique Internationale AGI for over 25 years, I have built up a worldwide circle of top-class colleagues/friends, with whom I have standing connections. And many pleasa encounters. This membership influenced and enriche my life strongly. As a designer, but also as a person.

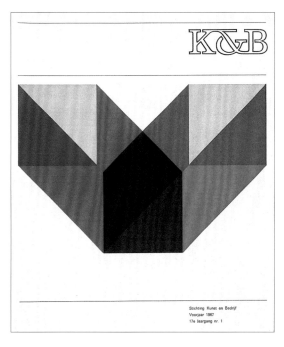

61

62

Campagne
de Souscription
Philips 1968

4 collections — 25 disques 30 cm

64

斯楚克图 ´68 陶瓷车间．商标
Ceramic workshop Struktuur '68, logotype

65

66

68

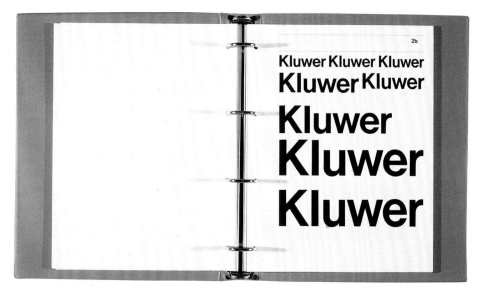

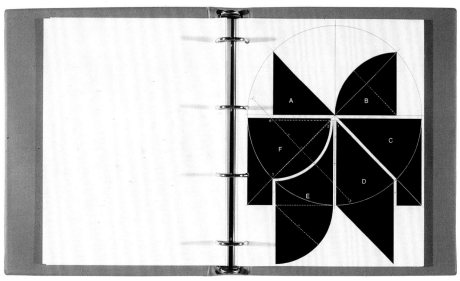

69

70

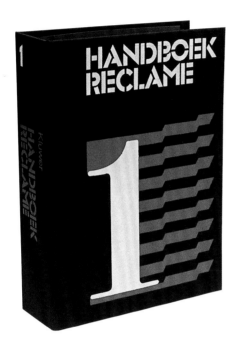

programma
kunst 10-daagse
1970
amsterdam

cisca

72

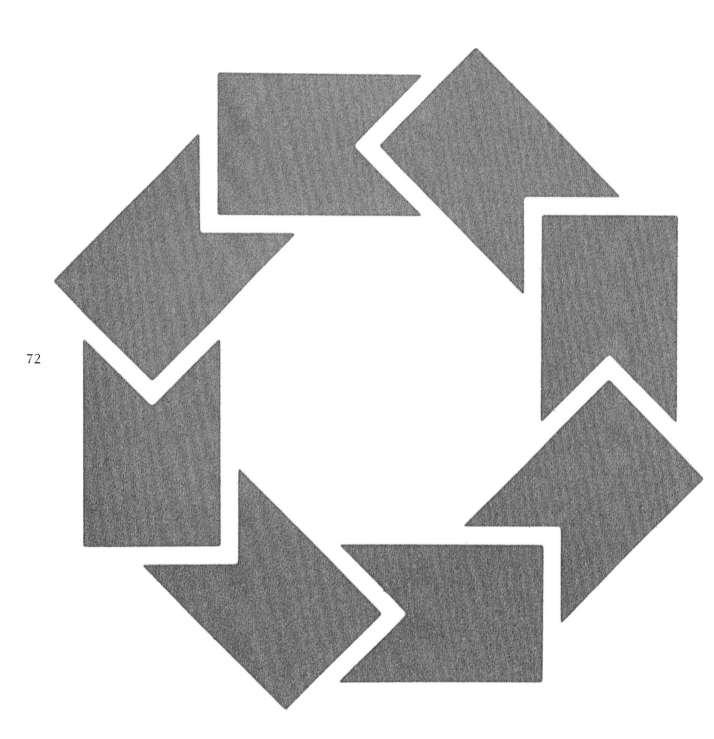

发内斯子公司，商标，1968/1974
Furness subsidiaries, logotypes 1968/ 1974

74

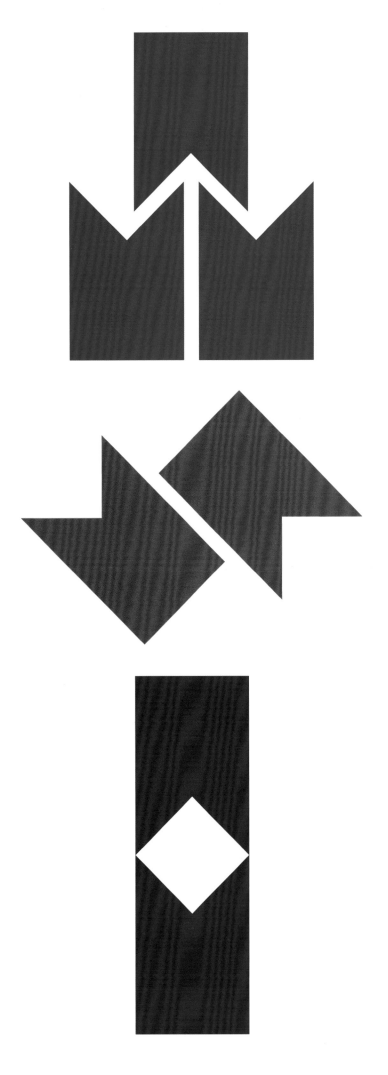

We are partners in:

Europe Container Terminus nv, Rotterdam

Rotterdam Fruit Pier nv, Rotterdam

Associated Offshore Supply & Transport
Services, Rotterdam.

76

Furness nv
Jaarverslag 1976

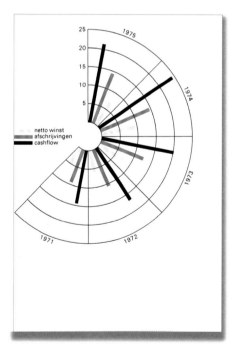

发内斯的港口，1968
Furness Harbours, 1968

发内斯的航运业，1970
Furness Shipping, 1970

发内斯的后勤，公路运输（现在用作控股公司标识）
Furness Logistics, road transport (present use of the holding logotype)

78

发内斯的后勤，公路运输（现在用作控股公司标识）
Furness Logistics, road transport (present use of the holding logotype)

AAB 爱因德霍温，医院承包人，商标，1969
AAB Eindhoven, hospital contractors, logotype 1969

79

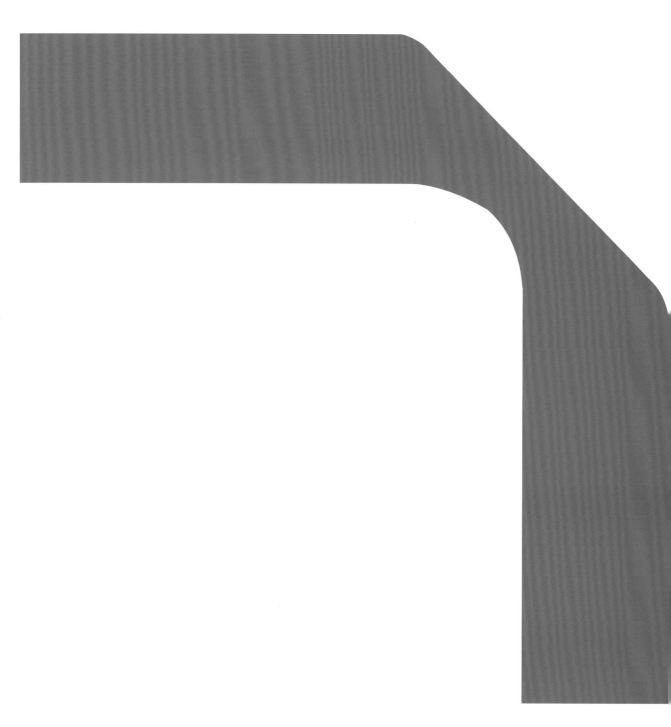

80

兰斯塔德雇佣服务的商标，1967
Logotype for Randstad employment services, 1967

81

兰斯塔德员工招募，展览摊位，1968
Randstad staff recruitment, exhibition stand 1968

82

兰斯塔德员工招募，展览摊位，1968
Randstad staff recruitment, exhibition stand 1968

At full speed in the

70's

七十年代全速前进

84

兰斯塔德总部，艺术品，1974
Randstad Head Quaters, art object, 1974

86

兰斯塔德总部，艺术品，1974
Randstad Head Quaters, art object, 1974

兰斯塔德新年贺卡，照片和设计，1974
Randstad New Years' greeting cards, 1974; photography and design

    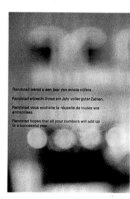

兰斯塔德新年贺卡，照片和设计，1974
Randstad New Years' greeting cards, 1974; photography and design

88

兰斯塔德表面字阿姆斯特丹分公司, 1974
Randstad facade lettering Amsterdam branch office, 1974

兰斯塔德分公司的隔离墙，1972
Randstad separation wall in a branch office, 1972

89

兰斯塔德分公司的隔离墙，1972
Randstad separation wall in a branch office, 1972

90

兰斯塔德新年海报，1975
Randstad New Years' poster, 1975

prettige dagen
en al het goede voor het
nieuwe jaar
randstad uitzendbureau

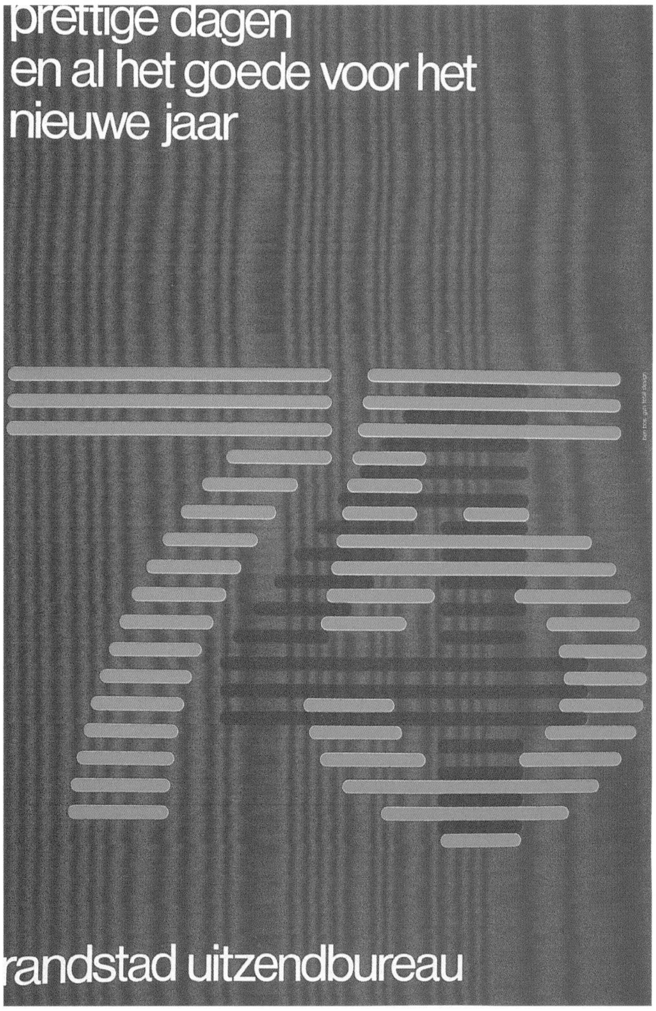

92

比利时 "劳工之间" 的商标，兰斯塔德子公司，1972
Logotype for Interlabor Belgium, a Randstad subsidiary, 1972

兰斯塔德万年历，1973
Randstad perpetual calendar, 1973

兰斯塔德万年历，1973
Randstad perpetual calendar, 1973

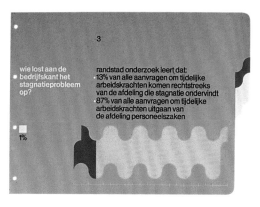

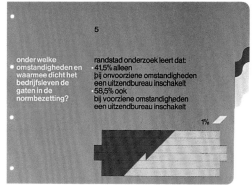

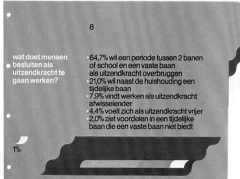

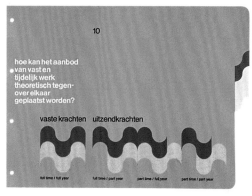

兰斯塔德阿姆斯特丹分公司的艺术品，1975
Randstad art object for Amsterdam branch office 1975

96

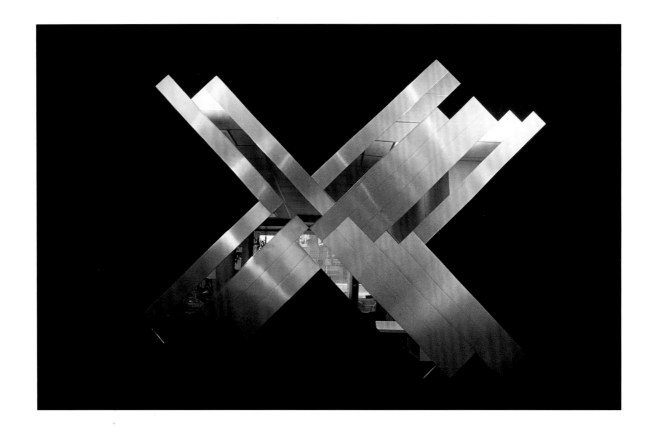

兰斯塔德阿姆斯特丹分公司的艺术品，1975
Randstad art object for Amsterdam branch office 1975

兰斯塔德客户杂志，1972，1974
Randstad client magazine, 1972, 1974

兰斯塔德总部，隔离墙，1971
Randstad headquarters, seperation wall. 1971

98

兰斯塔德总部，隔离墙，1971
Randstad headquarters, seperation wall. 1971

道德与审美：
我的职业思考

选择平面设计作为职业意味着设计者应该努力发掘他（或她）的真正职业态度，一个个人的"指导职业生涯的方法"。年轻的学生面临几个平面风格和不同的的设计方法。所以当他们认真地操作时，他们不得不确定他们的审美和道德价值观。

五十年代中期，当我来到这一职业舞台时，这还是一个相当年轻的领域。在阿姆斯特丹平面设计高中，我的第一个老师——现在年纪很大了——坚信经典的印刷法；这方面他从没有改变想法。但当我看到和经历了阿姆斯特丹战后环境后，我越来越被现代主义所吸引。在我们国家设计的真实场面充满了"新的声音"：像威尔·赛德伯格，阿姆斯特丹斯特德里奇克市立现代艺术博物馆的指导和设计者，简·范·丘伦，一份重要文化周刊的艺术指导，威姆·克罗威尔和高良乐（音）（两人合开一间内部装饰和展览设计工作室）这些人对设计和审美有一种新鲜和解放的看法。当然，在荷兰还有更多设计品质供欣赏。

在里埃特维尔德学院我参加了五年的晚班学习，我的绝大多数老师在设计和教育方法上坚定地信仰包豪斯——著名的现代"艺术大学"运动——创立于1919年，1933年被希特勒的纳粹分子关闭（太会革新了！）。皮特·布拉汀戈，纽约普拉特学院设计教授，同时也是他父亲的斯第恩朱克里奇·德·炯公司的印刷厂（在荷兰蒂尔弗逊）的设计画廊的主管，发起了一次展览会，内容是瑞士和国际风格的"气候"。他又出版了他的有价值的、常常带有他的经验的杂志"克瓦查特布拉登"。和这些人在一起，我感到真的在家一样。我的设计方面的杰出人物的圈子对于我找到我自己的职业方向起到了决定性的作用。

我力争用清晰和直接的视觉表达来反映客户的信息，没有任何有妨碍的（视觉）"杂音"。我发现，平面设计者的一个主要的义务是提供易读的作品。我的工具多数是无衬线字体；事实上，我最喜欢的只有很小的范围：阿克兹登兹·格罗台斯克，海尔维提卡，夫图拉——以及后来的弗鲁提克。我偏爱德·斯谛吉尔运动的基色方案，像画家冯·德斯伯格和蒙缀安，而不是使用合成色。事实上，我从来没有完全满意过潘通PMS印刷色。我很高兴能在工作时有时候使用更精致更强烈的HKS和DIC彩色墨水。我的大多数商标，当然是那些近年来的，很容易看懂——几乎能自我解释。我不追随时尚潮流，而更依靠我对于现在的感觉和对于未来的直觉。这使我能创作经久而且经常成为经典的商标。

谈到我的工作方式，我的符合我的思想的工作方式，我不得不作一个坦白。我工作得非常快。计划一宣布，我的思考进程就开始了。当我掌握了真实的基本情况的那一刻起，我就知道我该制作些什么了——这几乎已经成为定律了。我制作了一两幅草图，然后我把它们放大到要求的尺寸。在计算机时代我不打算自己打电脑：我和一个电脑专家一起工作（利用他的知识、他的设备、他的最成熟的硬件和总是最新的软件）。我只是和他坐在一起口授我的想

法。人多数情况下，我甚至不用给他看画在纸上的草图。口授时，所有的东西都在我的脑海里。使用电脑的好处是在细节上容易改变想法。客户不像旧时那样得到我的最初版本，而是多方面深思熟虑的结果。

作为一个热衷于摄影的人，我经常为我的任务拍摄照片——我非常相信黑白照片的交流力量。彩色照片现在用作一些产品，甚至是最便宜的产品的广告。黑白照片有一种特别考究的品质，其重点完全在于物体的形状和实质，没有压倒一切的色彩所造成的注意力分散。这不意味着完全拒绝好的高质量的彩色摄影；但因彩色是现在的主流，反差较大的黑白照片显得高贵和特别吸引人。

在我的作品中，网格也成为主要手段。尽管那意味着我的作品在组织上有独特的形式，我不排斥使用吸引人的"装饰"；我的作品并不冷淡，也不严肃。我不认为网格是一种约束；如果必要的话，我可以把我自己从这种形式中解放出来。在我早年为全体设计而作的作品中，网格仍然很新奇，必须向我的客户解释，这些客户经常担心用网格来工作会引向愚钝且痕迹太过明显。我因此制作了一个16毫米的电影胶卷，向他们展示了相当简单的网格能变幻出无穷的可能性；我使用这种网格为我的客户德·比简科夫——荷兰最前列的百货公司——的小个子雇员每月制作作品。这显示出我能用网格来制作这么多不同的作品，如果一幅接一幅排列，能够很容易地绕赤道一圈。

我的作品的价值建立在设计作品的所有组成部分之间完美的平衡之上。这意味着作品的内容同凸版印刷色彩的使用及纸张的使用一样重要，印刷和装订的质量也是一样。我从来就不是一个使用昂贵手法的设计者。我的作品也从来不意味着成为我自己的声誉的一种塑像。我喜欢以诚实而易理解的方式致意于我的最终用户。我知道任何一种交际都总是与其他各种交际竞争着。我从来都不否认我自己的政治和道德信条。我不会为我的"敌人"工作，也不会为我不信任或不尊敬的人工作。对于我的职业选择如此职责方式常使我同我的客户保持长久的关系。

101

我在"全体设计"工作时的团队中有许多出色的同事和助手，他们和我在一起有很长时间了，我还欠他们一份尊敬。在他们以后的职业生涯和打算中，我还经常参与其中。我成为国际平面造型艺术国际同盟的成员已经有二十五年了，我已经建立了一个顶极同事和朋友的国际圈子，我同他们保持联系，并且常常邂逅。这一会员身份强有力地影响我，充实了我的生活——不仅仅是一个设计者，也是一个个人。

本·博斯

Ethics and esthetics:
my professional considerations

Choosing for a carreer in graphic design means that the designer should try to find his (or her) true professional attitude, a personal 'way of conducting the professional life'. Young students are confronted with several graphic styles and different design approaches. So when they take it seriously, they'll have to make up their mind about esthetic and ethical values.

When during the mid-fifties I entered the platform of this profession, it was still a rather young field of activity. My first teacher at the Amsterdam Graphic high school - an elderly gentleman by now - strongly believed in a classic approach of typography; he never changed his mind in this respect. But from what I saw and experienced in the Amsterdam post-war environment, I became more and more attracted to Modernism.The actual design scene in our country was full of 'a new sound': people like Wil Sandberg, the director/designer of the Amsterdam Stedelijk (Municipal) Museum of Modern Art, Jan van Keulen, the art director for an important cultural weekly, Wim Crouwel and Kho Liang Ie (who had a joined studio for interior and exhibition design) had a fresh and liberating vision on design and esthetics. And of course there was more design quality to admire in the Netherlands.

At the Rietveld Academy, where I studied in the evening classes for five years, the majority of my teachers were strong believers in the design and educational approach of the Bauhaus, the famous modern movement 'art university' that was founded in 1919 and was closed down by Hitler's Nazis in 1933 (Too progressive!). Pieter Brattinga, professor of design at the Pratt Institute in New York, and also the director of the design gallery at his father's Steendrukkerij de Jong & Co. printing house (at

Hilversum, the Netherlands), promoted with his exhibitions the design 'climate' of the Swiss and International Style. He also published his valuable and often experimental magazine 'Kwadraatbladen'. With these people I could really feel 'at home'. The circle of my design heros got more and more a consistency that was decisive for finding my own professional direction.

I would strive for clear and direct visual translations of the clients' messages, without any disturbing (visual) 'noise'. I find offering easy legibility a major obligation for a graphic designer. My tools would be mostly sans serif typefaces; as a matter of fact a very limited selection of those: Akzidenz Grotesk, Helvetica, Futura - and later Frutiger - as my favourites. I would prefer the primary colour scheme of the De Stijl movement, of painters like Van Doesburg and Mondriaan, rather than using secondary mixed colours. I have - as a matter of fact - never been fully satisfied with the Pantone PMS printing colours. I was very happy to have been able to work sometimes with the much more refined or stronger colours of HKS and DIC inks. The majority of my logotypes, certainly those of the later years, can be easily understood - are almost self-explicatory. I don't follow fashion or trends; I rather depend on my awareness about the present and my antenna for the future. This helped me to create logotypes that could have a long life and often became classics.

Thinking about the way I work, the way I reach my concepts, I have to make a confession. I work very fast. As soon as the project has been announced, my thinking process is on the move. It is almost a rule that I know what I want to make the very minute I have got the real briefing. I make

a sketch or two, which I then blow up to the required size. In the computerized age I did not decide to do the keyboard job myself: I work with an expert operator (use his knowlegde, his equipment, his state-of-the-art hardware and always up-dated software) and I just sit with him and dictate my ideas. In most cases I even don't confront the operator with a real sketch on paper. It's all in my head, when we start the dictation. The great advantage of the computer is however that nowadays I will change my mind more easily about details. The client does not get my first version -like in the old days- but one that has been reconsidered in various aspects.

Being a keen photographer myself, often taking myself the pictures I needed for my commissions - I strongly believe in the communicative power of black & white photography. Since colour pictures are nowadays used for advertising even the cheapest products, black & white can represent a special 'elite' quality, where the accent lies entirely on shapes and the essence of the subject itself, without a distraction by often overwhelming colours. This does not mean a complete denial of good, high quality colour photography; but as colours are now 'mainstream', contrastful black & white has for me a kind of noblesse and special attractiveness.

The grid has been a dominating tool in my work as well. Although that meant that my works have a distinct form of organisation, I do not exclude the use of attractive 'ornaments'; my works are not cold or severe. Nor do I see the grid as an absolute straightjacket; if necessary I liberate myself from its pattern. In the early years of my work at Total Design grids were still a novelty and had to be explained to clients, who often feared that working with grids would lead to dull, too obvious design solutions. I then made a 16mm movie that showed them the really infinite possibilties of a rather simple grid, which I used for the small-sized employee's monthly for my client De Bijenkorf, the leading Dutch department stores. It showed that I could make so many page variations that they would, being laid side by side, easily surround the whole length of the Equator.

The values of my designs depend on a perfect balance between all components of the designed product. This means that content of the text is as important as the typography or the use of colours and paper, as well as the quality of printing and binding. I was never a designer who chose for expensive solutions. My works were never meant to become a kind of statues for my own fame. I prefer to address the final user in an honest, easily understandable way. I am always aware of the fact that any piece of communication is constantly in competition with many other pieces. I never denied my own political or ethical convictions. I would not work for 'the enemy', not for the kind of people I couldn't trust or respect. Choosing for such an approach of my professional responsibilty resulted quite often in longlasting friendly relationships with my clients.

Many good colleagues and assistants with whom I worked in my team at Total Design stayed with me for a long period; I owe them a lot of respect. I remained often involved in their later careers and plans. Having been a member of the Alliance Graphique Internationale AGI for over 25 years, I have built up a worldwide circle of top-class colleagues/friends, with whom I have standing connections. And many pleasant encounters. This membership influenced and enriched my life strongly. As a designer, but also as a person.

Ben Bos

103

104

科来科特，兰斯塔德的子公司，展览位置
Korrekt, a Randstad subsidiary; exhibition stand

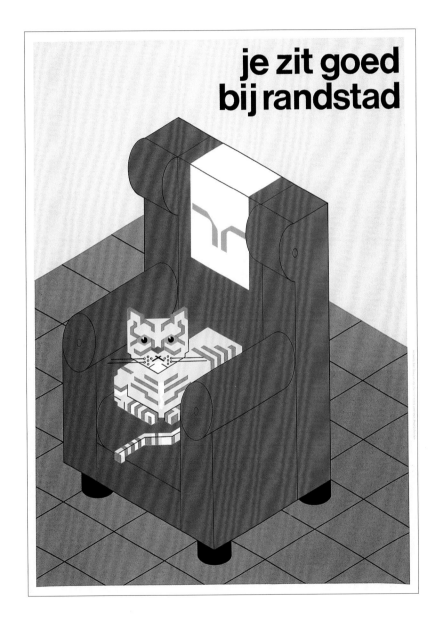

106

107

108

vereniging van zieken-
bejaarden- en andere
huisomroepen
hilversum
postbus 645

ZON，荷兰医院广播，商标，1977
ZON, Dutch hospital broadcasting, logotype, 1977

荷兰邮政，邮票议会间联盟和UNO，1970
Dutch Post, stamps Interparlementary Union and UNO, 1970

109

阿尔吉铭·汉德尔斯布拉德，日报，重新设计，1970
Algemeen Handelsblad, daily newspaper, restyling, 1970

NRC— 汉德尔斯布拉德日报，商标，1971
NRC—Handelsblad daily newspaper, logotype, 1971

111

国际追逐，安特卫普船运公司，商标和特征，1977
Chase International, shipping company Antwerp, logotype and identity, 1977

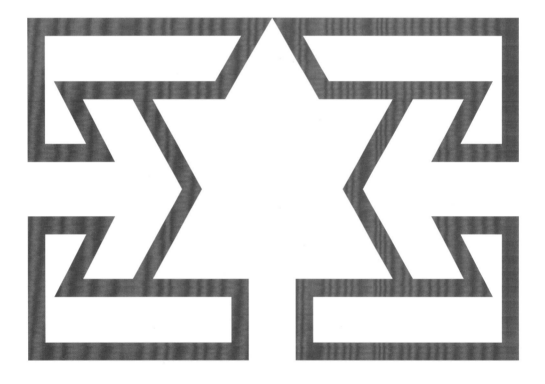

国际追逐，安特卫普船运公司，商标和特征，1977
Chase International, shipping company Antwerp, logotype and identity, 1977

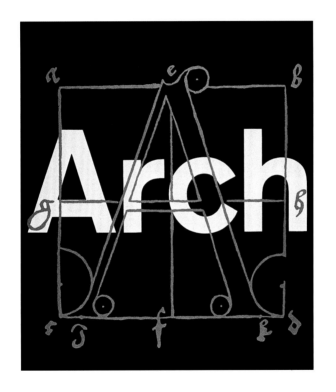

拱，建筑师和建筑工，商标，1975
Arch, architects and builders, logotype, 1975

国家投资银行的商标,海牙,1974
Logotype for The National Investment Bank, The Hague, 1974

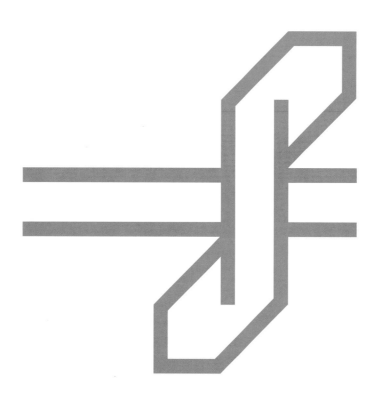

国家投资银行的商标,海牙,1974
Logotype for The National Investment Bank, The Hague, 1974

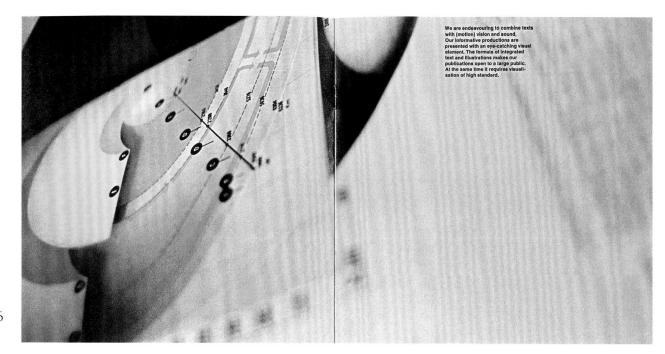

We are endeavouring to combine texts with (motion) vision and sound, Our informative productions are presented with an eye-catching visual element. The formula of integrated text and illustrations makes our publications open to a large public, At the same time it requires visualisation of high standard.

116

Spectrum Publishers, are general book-publishers for secondary school level and upwards. Among its publications you will find beautiful atlases and reference works, on all sorts of subjects (a.o. animal life) together with pocketbook and paperback series in the fiction and non-fiction field. Spectrum publications reach up to and include an academic market in its Aula academic pocketbook and paperback series. The IVR artwork is one of the essentials of the completely new Spectrum Encyclopedia produced by Spectrum Amsterdam for the international market. Together with the text, the colour photography and the computer software, composing elements of the encyclopedia conception, it gives the user ample visual insight and quick detailed reference.

阿姆斯特丹创造团队，商标，1972
Amsterdam Creative Team, logotype,1972

118

HVO "求助纸夹", 1980
HVO 'begging folder', 1980

120

HVO "求助纸夹", 1980
HVO 'begging folder', 1980

121

HVO "母亲与孩子之家" 运动, 1974
HVO campaign Home for Mothers and Children, 1974

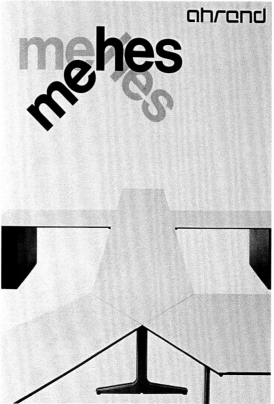

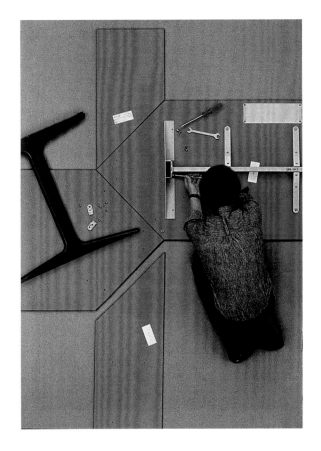 

阿赫恩德 · 美荷斯家具介绍小册子，1972
Introduction brochure Ahrend Mehes furniture, 1972

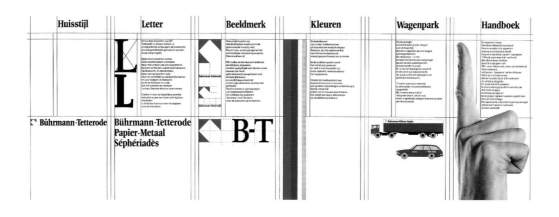

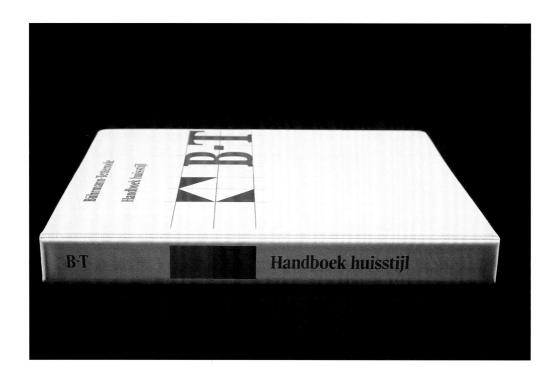

124

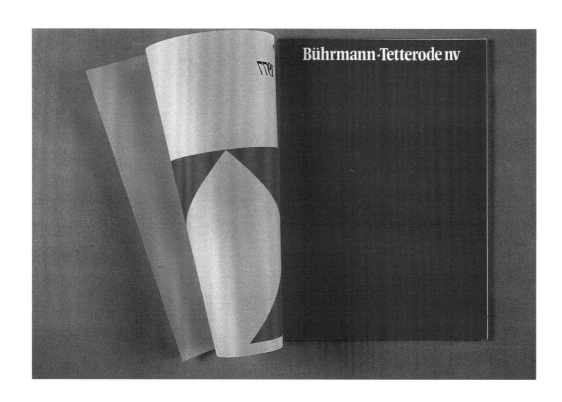

赫曼－特塔罗德，公司设计，1975
Jhrmann-Tetterode, corporate design, 1975

赫曼－特塔罗德（纸张批发和平面造型提供）设计手册，1975
Jhrmann-Tetterode (wholesale paper and graphic supplies) design manual, 1975

赫曼－特塔罗德，报告 1987
Jhrmann-Tetterode, report 1987

耐特威克 3 安全；兰斯塔德子公司，商标，1976
Netwerk 3 Security; a Randstad subsidiary. Logotype, 1976

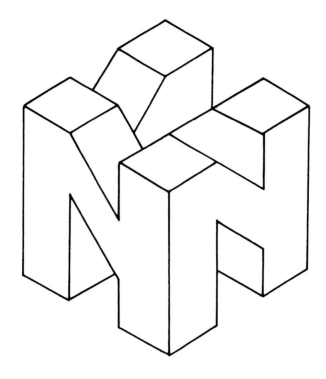

多罗敦市，商标，1975
City of Dronten, logotype, 1975

126

多罗敦市，商标，1975
City of Dronten, logotype, 1975

多罗敦市，小册子，1975
City of Dronten, brochure, 1975

多罗敦市，T-恤衫，1975
City of Dronten, T-shirt, 1975

128

德古鲁依斯特公路运输，1971
deGruyter road transport, 1971

德古鲁依斯特公路运输，1971
deGruyter road transport, 1971

德古鲁依斯特，牛奶，1972
deGruyter, milk, 1972

德古鲁依斯特，巧克力条，1972
deGruyter, chocolate bars, 1972

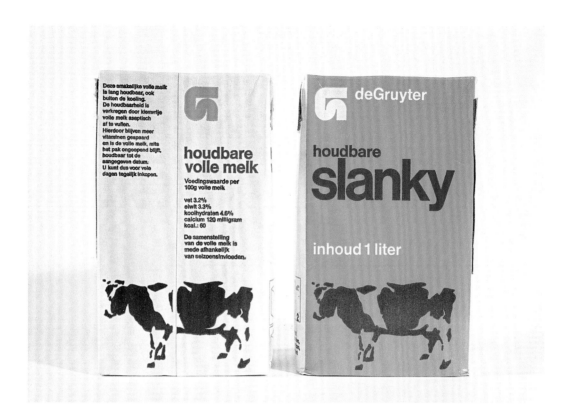

130

德古鲁依斯特，糕点，1972
deGruyter, pastry box, 1972

德古鲁依斯特，美乃滋（蛋黄酱），1972
deGruyter mayonnaise, 1972

德古鲁依斯特，泡菜，1972
deGruyter, sauerkraut, 1972

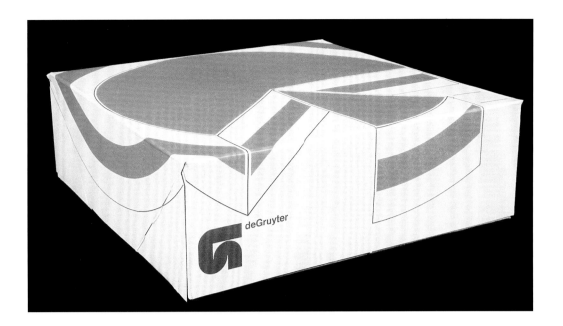

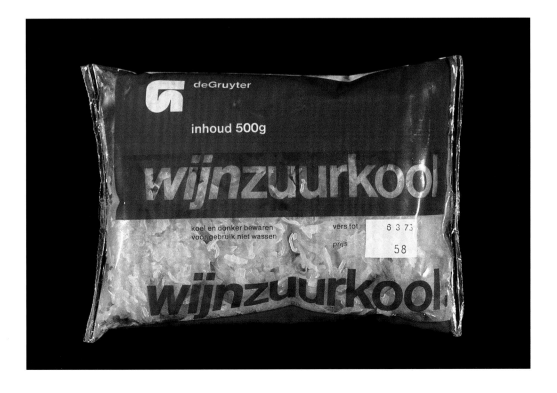

132

特威季恩斯特拉古德，管理顾问，商标，1977
TwijnstraGudde, management consultants, logotype, 1977

B&G 围栏制造者的商标，1978
Logotype B&G fencing manufacturers, 1978

133

B&G 围栏制造者的商标，1978
Logotype B&G fencing manufacturers, 1978

简特吉·德·古德，糕点，公司特征，1976
Jantje de Goede, pastries, corporate identity, 1976

简特吉·德·古德，先锋，1976
Jantje de Goede, van, 1976

134

简特吉·德·古德，糕点，公司特征，1976
Jantje de Goede, pastries, corporate identity, 1976

简特吉·德·古德，先锋，1976
Jantje de Goede, van, 1976

简特吉·德·古德，机器色彩设计，1978
Jantje de Goede, colour scheme for machines, 1978

136

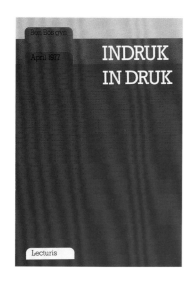

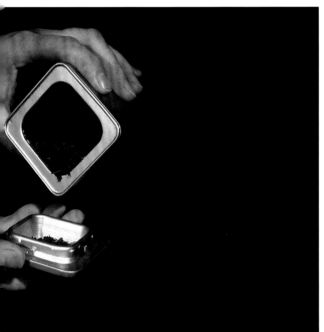

138

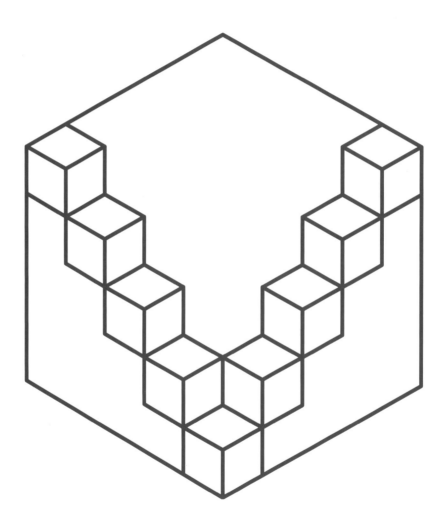

More in the

80's

八十年代更多

140

舞蹈海报，1983
Dance poster, 1983

141

142

纽 · 弗勒登伯格，阿姆斯特丹，老年之家，公司和内部设计／顾问，1980
Nieuw Vredenburgh, Amsterdam, old people's home, corporate and interior design/consultancy, 1980

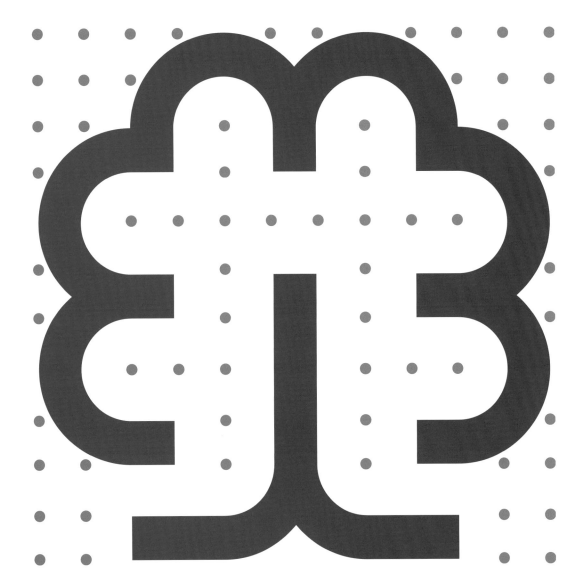

145

阿尔·伏太控股，迪拜；商标建议（未采纳），1982
Al Futtaim Holding Cy., Dubai; proposal for logotype (not used), 1982

146

兰斯塔德海报，1980
Randstad poster, 1980

147

GSI 法国（清洗）的商标，兰斯塔德子公司，1980
Logotype GSI France (Cleaning), a Randstad subsidiary, 1980

148

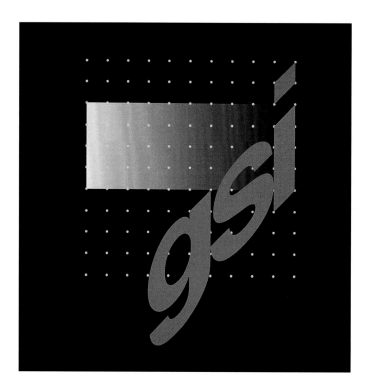

兰斯塔德的海报"税",1982
Randstad poster 'taxes', 1982

兰斯塔德的海报"税",1982
Randstad poster 'taxes', 1982

150

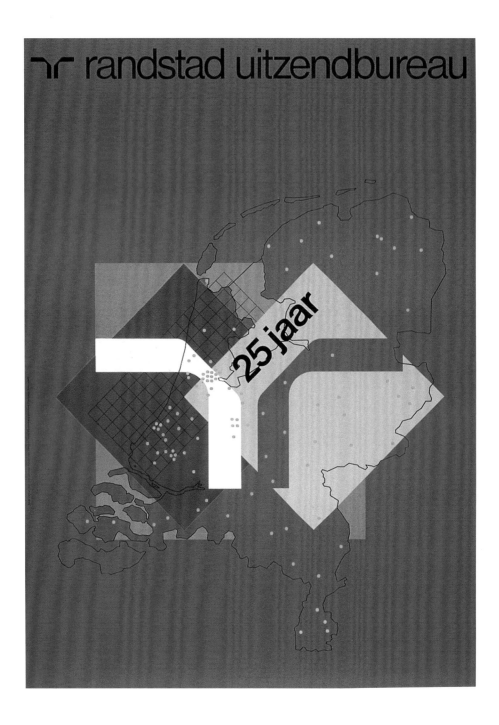

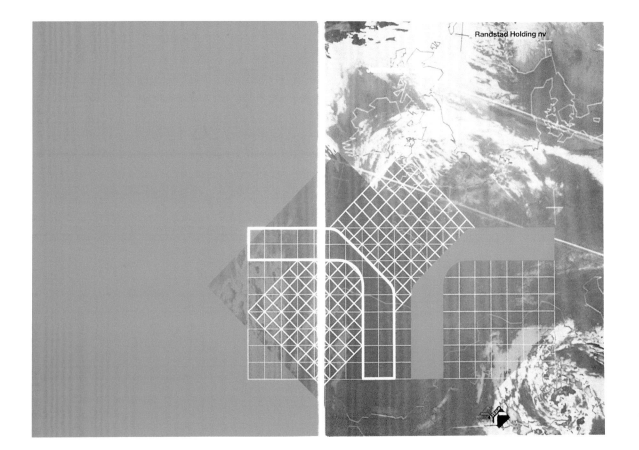

151

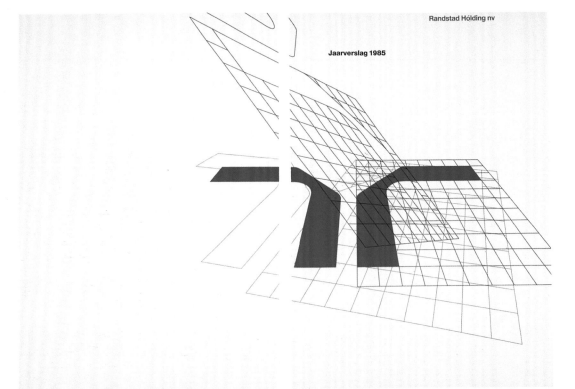

Jaarverslag 1985

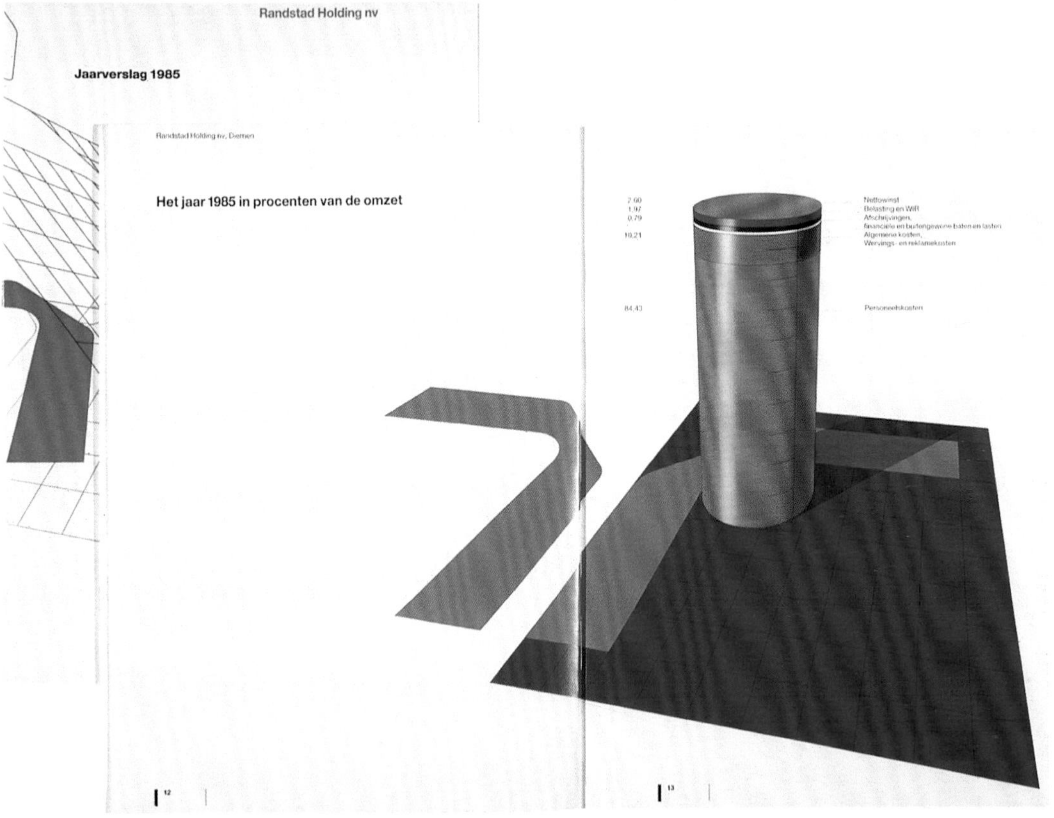

Randstad Holding nv
Jaarverslag 1985
Randstad Holding nv, Diemen
Het jaar 1985 in procenten van de omzet
2,60 Nettowinst
1,97 Belasting en WIR
0,79 Afschrijvingen, financiële en buitengewone baten en lasten
10,21 Algemene kosten, Wervings- en reklamekosten
84,43 Personeelskosten
12
13

154

Haben Sie
auch Arbeit für
Studenten?

Ja

Auch außerhalb der Semesterferien!

156

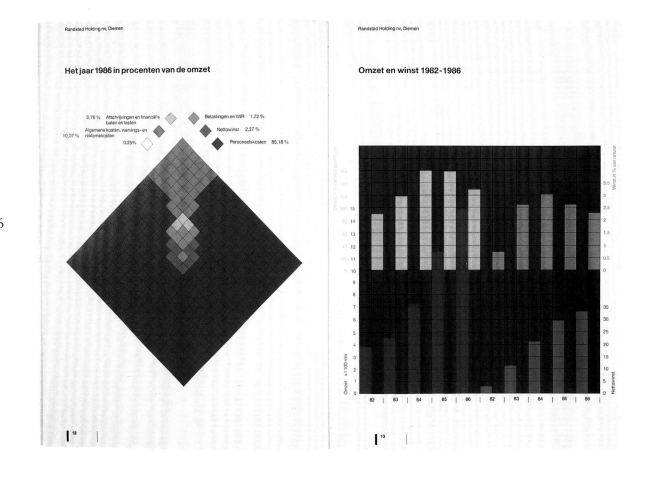

"包装兰斯塔德的五层建筑", 1987; 那时一个全新的主意
'Wrapping 5 floors of a Randstad building', 1987; at that time a completely new idea

157

"包装兰斯塔德的五层建筑", 1987; 那时一个全新的主意
'Wrapping 5 floors of a Randstad building', 1987; at that time a completely new idea

158

159

160

兰斯塔德总部，建筑上的文字，1988
Randstad HQ, architectural lettering, 1988

兰斯塔德接待员区，墙面设计 1988
Randstad receptionist area, wall design 1988

兰斯塔德海报：比利时二十年，1989
Randstad poster: 20 years in Belgium, 1989

兰斯塔德海报：比利时二十年，1989
Randstad poster: 20 years in Belgium, 1989

《为兰斯塔德工作的摄影师》，1989
Book 'Photographers at work for Randstad', 1989

163

《为兰斯塔德工作的摄影师》，1989
Book 'Photographers at work for Randstad', 1989

科来科特展览位置，1987
Korrekt exhibition stand, 1987

科来科特小册子，1987
Korrekt brochure, 1987

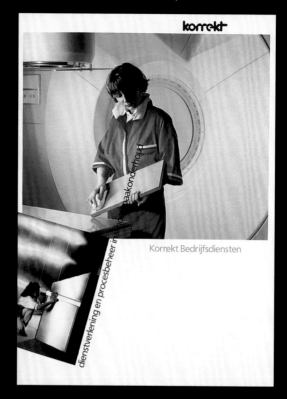

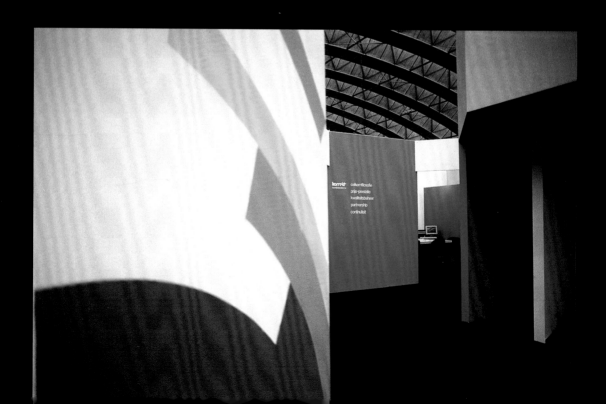

赫特·巴鲁尔，日报，重新设计，1984
Het Parool, daily newspaper, restyling, 1984

卡佩勒·安·登·依及塞尔市，荷兰，商标，1980
City of Capelle aan den IJssel, Holland, logotype, 1980

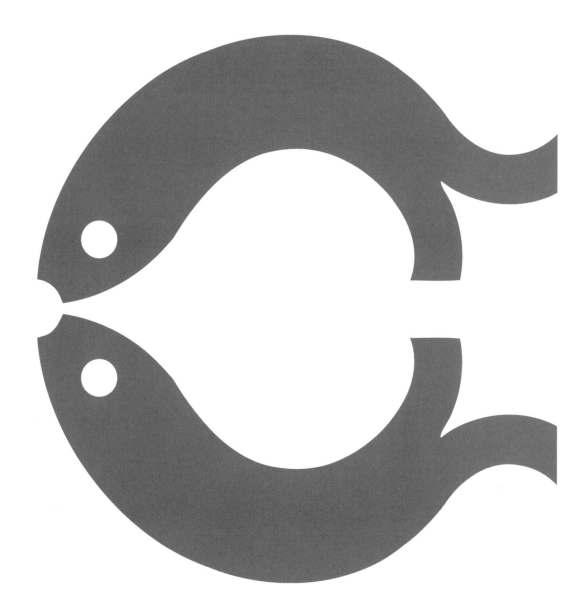

166

卡佩勒·安·登·依及塞尔市，荷兰，商标，1980
City of Capelle aan den IJssel, Holland, logotype, 1980

卡佩勒，市政厅的路线安排，1982
Capelle, routing for cityhall, 1982

168

卡佩勒，垃圾卡车，1980
Capelle, garbage truck, 1980

卡佩勒，城市码头的商标
Capelle, logo on city wharf, 1984

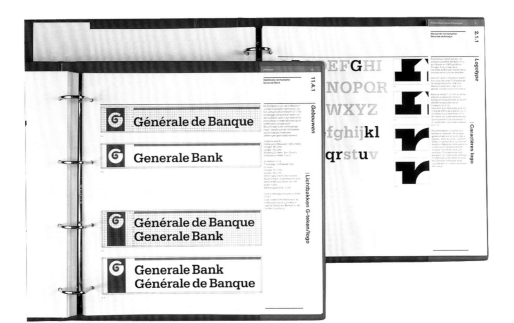

 **Generale Bank**

杰纳拉勒银行，布鲁塞尔，公司设计
Generale Bank, Brussels, corporate design

170

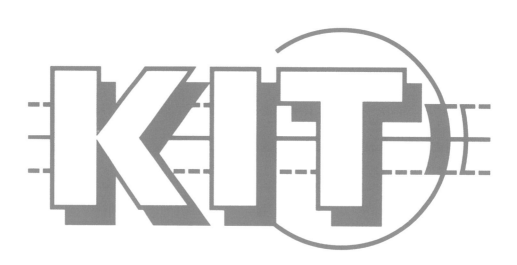

克雷迪托·因德斯垂阿尔·萨多，卡利亚里（意大利），商标建议，1988
Credito Industriale Sardo, Cagliari (It.), logo proposal, 1988

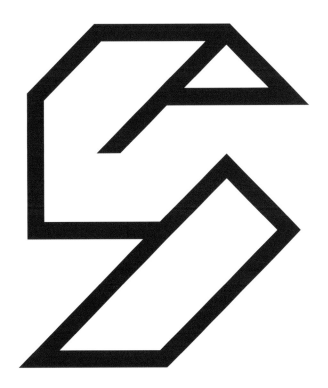

克雷迪托·因德斯垂阿尔·萨多，卡利亚里（意大利），商标建议，1988
Credito Industriale Sardo, Cagliari (It.), logo proposal, 1988

172

174

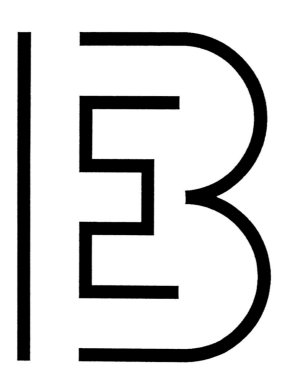

尼德兰登·范，1870，保险；建筑上的文字，1990
Nederlanden van 1870, insurances; architectural lettering, 1990

176

尼德兰登·范，1870，保险；建筑上的文字，1990
Nederlanden van 1870, insurances; architectural lettering, 1990

Twosome harvest

90's

九十年代两人收获

178

FORMatie2

179

180

NEDERLAND

FEPAPOST 94
17 t/m 23 oktober

Luscinia
svecica

+70
80c

Blauwborst

Ben Bos AGI BNO
Amsterdam, the Netherlands

+70
80c
NEDERLA

Commission:
Series of 3 stamps for the Dutch Post 1994

Subject:
FEPAPOST 94 International Stamp Exhibition
The Hague

OBSERVATOIRE INTERNATIONAL DES PRISONS

BenBosagi

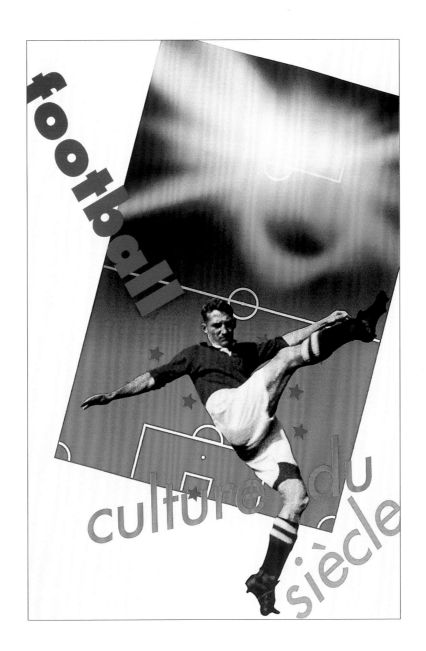

183

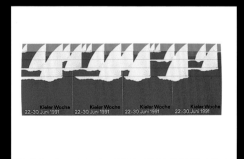

基勒·沃什，年度帆船比赛；国际设计竞赛，1991
Kieler Woche, annual sailing sports event; international design competition, 1991

斯帕恩伍德放风筝节海报，1999
Poster kite-flying event Spaarnwoude, 1999

斯帕恩伍德放风筝节海报，1999
Poster kite-flying event Spaarnwoude, 1999

186

NAGO，荷兰档案平面设计者，第二个商标，1996
NAGO, Netherlands Archive Graphic Designers, second logo, 1996

188

埃森，反对童工运动的海报；摄影艾迪·颇斯苏玛·德·波尔，1998，1999
Essen, poster for campaign against child labour; photography Eddy Posthuma de Boer ,1998, 1999

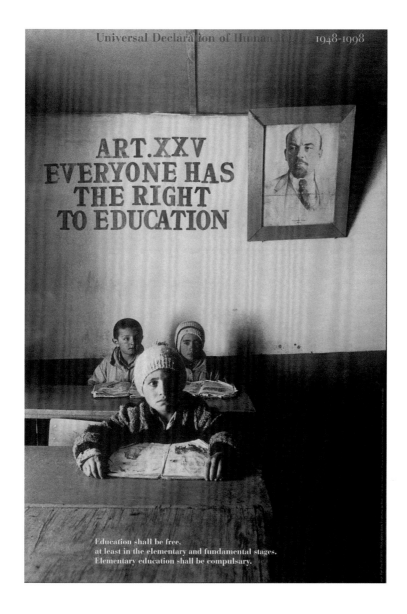

189

兰斯塔德USA，计划日历，1994
Randstad USA, planning calendar, 1994

兰斯塔德USA，本月员工奖，1994
Randstad USA, Employee of the Month awards, 1994

190

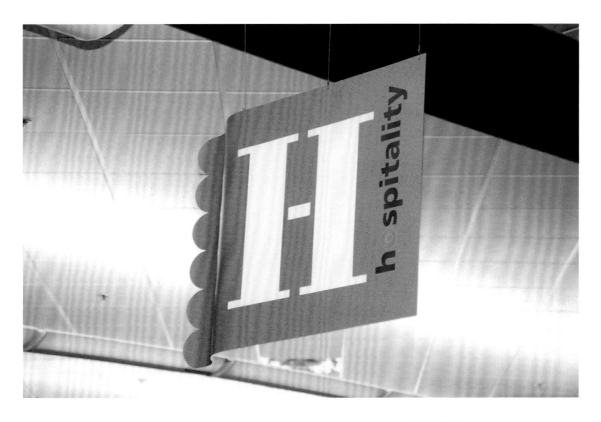

兰斯塔德USA，亚特兰大内部设计和照片墙，1996
Randstad USA, interior design and photowalls Atlanta, 1996

192

兰斯塔德USA，亚特兰大内部设计和照片墙，1996
Randstad USA, interior design and photowalls Atlanta, 1996

194

荷兰档案平面设计者，艾尔伏海报展，1996
Netherlands Archive Graphic Designers, exhibition poster Elffers, 1996

美荷斯小册子，艺术导向和设计，1993
Mehes brochure, art direction and design, 1993

赫恩德百年展海报，1996
ster Ahrend centennial exhibtion, 1996

赫恩德百年展，馆长本·博斯，1996；梅杰＆范·格温设计
rend centennial exhibition, curator Ben Bos, 1996; designers Meijer & Van Gerwen

美荷斯家具小册子，1998
Brochure Mehes furniture, 1998

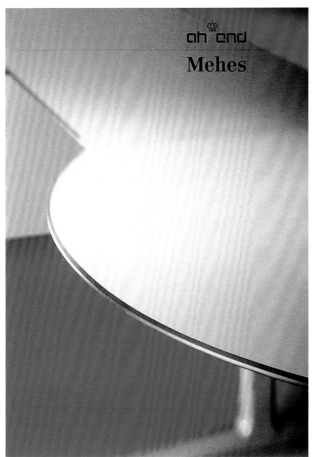

197

198

斯特阿赫恩德家具展邀请卡，1999
itation card for Ahrend furnitue show Manchester, 1999

姆·奎斯特的家具设计邀请卡，阿赫恩德，1998
itation card for presentation of Wim Quist furniture, Ahrend, 1998

台玻璃板小册子，1998
chure desk screens, 1998

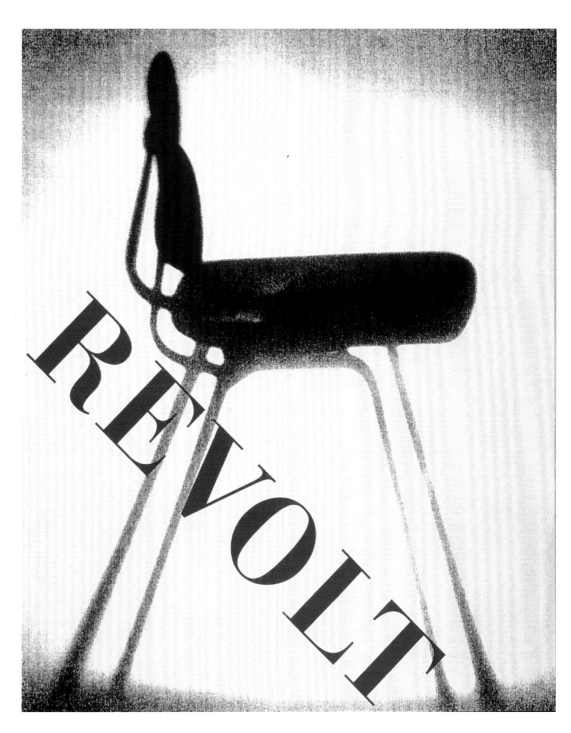

199

新当选的阿赫恩德反对派主席的邀请函，1993
Invitation leaflet for the remake of the Ahrend Revolt chair, 1993

图书在版编目（CIP）数据

　　本·博斯／（荷）博斯著；甘宜龙译．－上海：上海
三联书店，2006.9
　　（三联国际平面设计大师作品系列）
　　ISBN 7-5426-2377-X

　　Ⅰ.本…　　Ⅱ.①博…②甘…　　Ⅲ.平面设计－作品
集－荷兰－现代　Ⅳ.J534

中国版本图书馆 CIP 数据核字（2006）第 101148 号

本·博斯

主　　编／余秉楠
译　　者／甘宜龙

责任编辑／范峤青
封面设计／范峤青
版面设计／焦　燕
监　　制／林信忠
责任校对／张大伟

出版发行／上海三联书店
　　　（200031）中国上海乌鲁木齐南路 396 弄 10 号
　　　http://www.sanlianc.com
　　　E-mail.shsanlian@yahoo.com.cn
印　　刷／上海精英彩色印务有限公司
版　　次／2006 年 9 月第 1 版
印　　次／2006 年 9 月第 1 次印刷
开　　本／889 × 1194　1/16
印　　张／12.75

书　　号：ISBN 7-5426-2377-X/J·83
定　　价：148.00 元